TRIAL

Trial

Book 3 of the Search for Truth Series

Ruth Chesney

RITCHIE
John Ritchie Publishing

40 Beansburn, Kilmarnock, Scotland

ISBN-13: 978 1 910513 91 0

40 Beansburn, Kilmarnock, Scotland

www.ritchiechristianmedia.co.uk

This is a work of fiction. The characters, incidents and dialogues are products of the author's imagination and are not to be construed as real. Any resemblance to actual events or persons, living or dead, is entirely coincidental.

Typeset by John Ritchie Ltd., Kilmarnock
Printed by Bell & Bain, Glasgow

For Uncle Thomas and Auntie Margaret.
Everyone needs a Cherryhill Farm in their life.
Ballycraigagh was mine.

Chapter One

"Seb! *Move!*" Uncle Matt yelled as five hundred kilos of Holstein bull charged across the yard. Seb grabbed the upper bar of the gate and vaulted over, his wobbly legs barely supporting him as he landed. He pressed against the wall, the ground vibrating beneath his feet. He was no longer able to see where the bull was, but knew that any second now the animal would launch himself at the gate. Seb only hoped the gate would hold and not be torn from its hinges. The bellowing and snorting came closer. Seb winced and braced himself, holding his length of blue alkathene pipe aloft, like a medieval knight in a sword fight.

The thundering hooves drew near, then abruptly stopped. The bull bellowed again. Seb frowned. If the sound was anything to go by, the animal seemed to have changed direction. Gingerly, Seb peered around the wall, and froze in horror. The bull had a new target in his sights. Head lowered, he pawed the ground once, then catapulted himself towards Uncle Matt. Matt turned and dashed for the gate on the other side of the yard, but the bull was too fast. He lifted and flung him against the pillar like a ragdoll, pinning him there and grinding his head against Matt's leg.

"*No!*" screamed Seb. He looked desperately around for help, but no one was in sight. He leaped back over the gate. If he didn't do something, Uncle Matt was going to die. The bull was in a frenzy. Wild. Angry. Seb approached, trembling, driven by desperation. Suddenly the animal backed away and Uncle Matt dropped to the ground in a crumpled heap. Was the bull moving away to renew his attack? Or was he now going to turn on Seb?

Seb breathed a silent prayer. He could hear his heart thudding in his chest and he took a deep breath. Surely the same God who could calm the wind and waves in ancient Israel could calm a raging bull in modern-day Northern Ireland!

The bull strolled into the middle of the yard, his anger spent like dandelion fluff on a windy day. Seb glanced at Uncle Matt. He wasn't moving and, more than anything, Seb wanted to go straight to him. But he needed to get the bull out of the way. He took another deep breath and walked towards him, suppressing the urge to rush. The last thing he needed was to startle the animal.

The bull headed towards the cowshed, paused to sniff one of the heifers in the adjoining enclosure, then sauntered into his pen. A prayer of thanksgiving on his lips, Seb quickly rammed the bar of the gate into the socket before dashing out of the shed and across the yard. He dreaded to think what he would find.

"Uncle Matt? Can you hear me?" Seb reached down to touch his uncle's shoulder. He cringed at the cuts and grazes on his face.

His uncle groaned.

"You're alive!" Seb exclaimed.

"Barely," Matt ground out between gritted teeth. "My leg..."

Seb glanced down at his uncle's leg. Was it lying at a strange angle? "Stay there. I'll go for Aunt Karen."

"Not moving anywhere anytime soon," he moaned.

Seb shook his head in self-rebuke. "Of course not."

As Seb burst through the back door, Karen jumped. "Goodness, Seb! Is something wrong?"

"It's Uncle Matt... The new bull... His leg..."

Karen turned pale and the vegetable peeler clattered into the sink. She dashed through the door, wiping her hands on her apron as she sprinted across the yard.

"What's wrong with Daddy?" Martha, Seb's little cousin, asked as he prepared to follow his aunt.

"He's–he fell," Seb said.

"I want to see him," she said, worry clouding her big blue eyes.

Seb shook his head. The last thing Martha needed was to see her daddy in extreme pain. "I think you should stay here for now. You can see him later."

A fat bottom lip protruded and wobbled.

"I need you to look after Glen," Seb said hurriedly.

The lip stopped trembling and Martha's shoulders lifted. "I'll go and get him."

Seb put a hand on her shoulder. "Stay there. I'll get him."

He dashed across the yard and unclipped the chain from the little dog's collar. The dog bounced excitedly around Seb. He hadn't appreciated being tied up, but Uncle Matt hadn't wanted an excitable pup around when he was cleaning out the bull's pen. When Seb reached the house, Martha was on the step, pulling on her pink wellies. "It's okay, Martha. You can look after Glen in the kitchen today."

Her eyes widened. "In the kitchen?" she repeated. "But Mummy doesn't let Glen into the kitchen!"

Seb tried for what he hoped was a reassuring smile. "It'll be fine for once," he said. "Your mummy won't mind."

Martha looked unsure. "Well, if I get into trouble, I'm blaming you!"

Seb winked at her. "That's okay. I'll explain." He opened the door and pushed the black and white collie inside. Martha followed and he closed the door behind them both. He raced back across the yard to where Uncle Matt was still lying, Aunt Karen kneeling beside him.

She looked up as Seb approached, a worried look on her face. "We need an ambulance," she said. "There's no way we can lift him, and I don't think I want to. His leg doesn't look good."

Seb nodded. He hoped there wasn't internal damage as well. That bull had been trying to kill him. He pulled his phone from his pocket, unlocked it and handed it to Aunt Karen. She straightened, took the phone and dialled 999.

The ambulance seemed to take forever to arrive. Matt lay still, barely speaking, his face drawn. Aunt Karen sent Seb back to the house with instructions to phone Mrs Harvey to ask her to bring home Lavinia, their eldest daughter, and take Martha back with her. She'd likely need to keep her overnight. Lavinia had been spending the first day of the autumn half-term holidays with her friend, Rebekah Harvey, and had planned to stay for dinner. Now she would be needed to help Seb with the milking instead.

Finally, the ambulance pulled into the yard. Aunt Karen must have waved to the driver, as the yellow and green vehicle turned and reversed to where Uncle Matt was lying.

Martha joined Seb at the back door. "Is Daddy going in an ambulance?" she asked. The worried look was back on her face. Glen barked and pulled at one of her socks with his teeth.

How much should he tell Martha? "Yes, your daddy needs to go to hospital to make sure he's okay." Seb hoped he wasn't stretching the truth. He ushered Martha and Glen back into the kitchen. Seb desperately wanted to be outside with Uncle Matt. He needed to know that his uncle *was* going to be okay.

He heard another vehicle drive into the yard and glanced out the kitchen window. It was Mrs Harvey with Lavinia. As the car pulled to a stop, Lavinia's door opened and she leaped out and ran down the yard. Then a light tap sounded at the back door and Mrs Harvey entered, followed by Rebekah.

As Martha looked up, they smiled. "Martha!" Mrs Harvey exclaimed. "So you're coming to stay with us."

Martha frowned and shook her blonde curls. "I think I prefer to stay at home, if you don't mind, Mrs Harvey."

Rebekah hid a smile beneath her hand and glanced at Seb. Sometimes Martha was more like an old lady than a four-year-old girl.

Mrs Harvey crouched down to speak to the little girl. "I know that, Martha, but I think you'll have good fun at our house. Remember, we have Glen's sister, Moss, and you can play with the dolls' house."

Martha's eyes lit up. "The big dolls' house? The one with a swimming pool?"

Mrs Harvey smiled. "That's the one. Now, will we go and find your pyjamas?" She took her by the hand and led her upstairs.

Seb turned to Rebekah. "Must be some dolls' house."

"It is." Glen batted her leg with his paw and she bent down to rub his ears. "It was mine first, then my sisters played with it." She looked up at Seb, sympathy showing in her blue eyes. "How's your uncle?"

Seb sighed. "It doesn't look good. He's alive, but there's definitely something up with his leg and I don't know what all else. That bull... " He shuddered, the vision of Uncle Matt being attacked still too fresh in his mind.

The door opened and Lavinia burst in. He could see traces of tears on her face. "The ambulance people want to talk to you, Seb. You saw what happened."

Seb headed back across the yard. The paramedics had lifted Uncle Matt into the ambulance, and Seb could see him lying on a trolley. Apart from the cuts and grazes, he looked even paler than before. Aunt Karen didn't look much better.

After he'd told the paramedics about the attack, he climbed into the ambulance to speak to his uncle.

"Thank you," Uncle Matt murmured.

Seb looked down at his strong uncle. "I'll be praying for you," Seb told him. "And don't worry about the milking – Vinnie and I will be fine."

An anxious look fleetingly passed across Uncle Matt's face, then he blinked.

"Right, we're ready to go," the grey-haired paramedic called. Seb stepped back out of the ambulance and waved. The doors shut and the vehicle moved off.

Aunt Karen sighed. She looked close to tears. Seb put an arm around her and she leaned into his embrace. "Oh, Seb," she breathed. "I don't know how we're going to cope."

Seb looked at her in alarm. Was Uncle Matt so ill that he was actually going to die?

Aunt Karen saw his concerned look and gave him a slight smile. "The Lord knows all about it. Keep praying, Seb." She straightened and walked briskly towards the house. "Now, I must see if Martha's ready and then hurry to the hospital. I'm sorry I haven't managed to get the dinner ready, but hopefully you can find something when the milking is done."

The milking was carried out in silence that evening. Every so often, Lavinia paused to dash away tears from her cheeks. Seb felt sick. He hated to think of Uncle Matt in pain, and it felt like torture, not knowing if he was going to be all right. What if Uncle Matt died? How would they ever manage? Seb suddenly felt close to tears himself and he took a deep breath. The cow nearest to him kicked the clusters off and Seb grabbed them, rinsed them off and replaced them. Even the cows were uneasy. They too seemed to sense that something terrible had happened.

The last cow left the parlour and Seb turned the parlour over to the wash-up setting. Lavinia grabbed the scraper and began to furiously scrape down where the cows had been standing.

"It's so unfair," she muttered. "Why should this happen to Dad, of all people?"

Seb frowned. He'd been the only other person in the yard when the bull had gone mad. Surely Vinnie wasn't thinking it would have been better if *he* had been attacked?

"I *hate* bulls," she went on. "Mean," she shoved the scraper across the concrete, "wicked... evil... hateful... *beasts!*" she finished, lifting the scraper and pounding it on the wall. She began to scream, beating the wall with all her might.

Seb watched, alarmed. Vinnie was going crazy! How on earth was he supposed to calm her down? “Vinnie…” he began hesitantly.

“Don’t talk to me,” she yelled. “Couldn’t you have warned him that the bull was there? Why didn’t you go and help him? You probably ran away and left him to deal with that bull on his own! It nearly killed him! In fact…” Her anger melted into a puddle. “Maybe he is going to die,” she finished, tears gathering in her eyes as she sank to the ground, the scraper falling with a clatter beside her. Unmindful of the cow dung, she sat with her head in her hands, shaking. Every so often she gave a loud sniff and wiped her eyes with her sleeve.

“Vinnie,” Seb said softly, “why don’t you go inside. I’ll finish off out here.” He was surprised when, after a moment, she staggered to her feet and left, still wiping her eyes.

Seb picked up the scraper and began where Lavinia had left off, but he struggled to take a deep breath due to the crushing weight in his chest. Finally, he set the scraper down and sat down on the steps, head in his hands. Unlike Lavinia, he had Someone to turn to when things got tough. He had a caring heavenly Father, One to whom he could pour out his heart. This was a very difficult day. No one knew what was ahead. To lose Uncle Matt was unthinkable. What could Seb do, but pray?

He bowed his head and closed his eyes.

Chapter Two

"I know it's not what we'd planned for the first week in our new house, Mum, but they need me here."

Mum's sympathetic sigh came clearly through the phone. "Seb, I know that. Of course you can stay at Cherryhill. I'm working every day this week anyway." She paused. "I do hope Matt's okay," she said, worry in her voice.

"So do I," replied Seb.

Aunt Karen hadn't been in touch since she'd left for the hospital. The tension in the air was palpable. Lavinia had grabbed the farming paper and was rapidly flicking through it. When she reached the last page, she held it upright and tapped it on the table in an attempt to straighten the edges, then began again. Half-eaten slices of toast lay on their plates. Seb took a sip of tea and grimaced. Stone cold. He stood up and began to clear the table. As he was carrying the pile of plates and cups to the sink, Lavinia's mobile rang. Seb startled, but managed to land the crockery onto the work surface before everything slid to the floor.

Lavinia snatched up the phone and swiped the screen to answer the call. "How's Dad?" she asked hurriedly.

"Put it on loud speak," hissed Seb. It could only be Aunt Karen.

Lavinia rolled her eyes at Seb. "One minute, Mum." She tapped the screen and set the phone on the table. "Go ahead. How is he?"

"He's stable." Aunt Karen sounded weary, but relieved. "Thanks be to God."

"So he's not going to... to... " Lavinia swallowed.

"He's going to be fine."

Lavinia and Seb looked at each other and grinned. Seb released a breath he didn't even realise he'd been holding. Uncle Matt was going to live!

"However," went on Aunt Karen, "he's got a long, long way to go. His femur is badly broken and he needs surgery. They might insert a metal rod."

"In his leg?" asked Seb. He couldn't remember which bone was the femur.

"Yes, his upper leg. He'll be in hospital for most of the week. He's feeling pretty sore all over and he's got lots of cuts and bruises, but thankfully there were no internal injuries. That's quite a miracle, the doctors said."

"So his broken leg is the worst injury?" Lavinia asked.

"That's right," replied Aunt Karen. "They have him on pain relief, so he's fairly comfortable for now. His surgery is scheduled for tomorrow morning."

Seb winced. He didn't even want to consider how they would go about inserting a metal rod into someone's leg.

"I'll be home later," Aunt Karen went on, "but I think you'd better head for bed. You need all the sleep you can get, and milking time comes early."

They said their goodbyes and Seb finished clearing up the dishes. He took the remnants of toast outside and gave them to Jess and Glen. Jess ate the toast, then pressed herself against his leg. She seemed to detect his sombre mood. Seb sank onto the step and put an arm around the sedate and wise older dog. Glen circled them, batting at Seb's shoulder with a big paw, before finally settling down and curling up at his feet.

Jess leaned closer and licked his cheek. Seb grinned wryly and rubbed the dog saliva away with his sleeve. Doggy kisses were all right, but he'd seen Jess's secret liking for cow dung.

The night was still and peaceful. The cows lowed softly in the shed, and the stars twinkled overhead. It was only this morning that Uncle Matt had collected him from the new house in town that Seb and Mum had moved to at the weekend, and taken him to Cherryhill Farm to help out. Who would have thought that, by the end of the day, Uncle Matt would be lying in hospital, facing surgery tomorrow? A verse from the Bible flitted into Seb's mind. *Do not boast about tomorrow, for you do not know what a day may bring forth.* How true!

His mind replayed the events of the day. The bull, rushing towards him and then turning to Uncle Matt. Could Seb have done anything differently? Was Lavinia right? Was he a coward, turning and running? He'd only done what he'd thought best at the time. He sighed and rubbed Jess's soft fur. At least he'd managed to get the bull back in the pen without further mishap.

"Why are you sitting out here in the dark?" Lavinia's voice came from the door.

Seb struggled to his feet. "Just... thinking. It's getting cold though. I'll be in soon."

He could see Lavinia shrug, the light from the hallway casting her as a silhouette. "I'm going to bed. See you in the morning."

Seb yawned as he pressed the button to start up the milking machine. He'd tossed and turned a lot and it seemed that when he finally fell asleep, it was time to get up. Lavinia looked about as well slept as he did.

"I wonder how Dad is this morning," she remarked as she let the first batch of cows into the milking parlour. "He's likely lying fretting about not doing any work. He isn't very good at being a patient, not that he's often sick."

"Do you think we'll be allowed to go and see him?" Seb asked, pulling on a pair of disposable gloves.

Lavinia shrugged. "I don't know what time his surgery is. It probably depends on that." She bit her lip. "I hope he won't have a long recovery period. We still have loads of cows to calve, and the TB test is coming up next week."

"TB test?" This was something new that Seb hadn't come across before.

"Tuberculosis. Every herd needs tested each year. The vet comes out and gives them a couple of wee injections in their necks and then comes back three days later to check if they've reacted or not."

"Reacted to the injections?"

"Yes, if they react to the bovine TB one, they have to be culled."

"Culled. You mean, like... " Seb paused. Surely not!

"Yep, slaughtered," Lavinia replied matter-of-factly. "It hasn't ever happened here, so hopefully we're okay this year too." She began to attach the clusters to the cows. "The only problem is that we have loads of dairy cows, not to mention the heifers and older calves. We need all the help we can get."

"What about the bull?" asked Seb.

Lavinia groaned. "I'd forgotten about him. He needs tested too, unless, of course, we get rid of him first."

"Your dad would hardly want to keep him."

Lavinia shook her head. "He's a good bull." She rolled her eyes and gave a mirthless laugh. "What I mean is, he's from a good bloodline, but Dad always says that if something is dangerous, it has to go, no matter what."

"Is there anyone who can help out while Uncle Matt's recovering?" he asked.

"Caleb can still help with morning milking," she said, turning slightly pink.

Seb let the row of cows out and hid a grin. His cousin had more than a passing interest in Rebekah's older brother, Caleb. Their attempts to be discreet weren't too successful and everyone knew the feeling was mutual.

"But he still has his job, and his own cattle to look after," she continued. Seb sobered. She was right. There was only so much time Caleb could spare. Tommy, the old neighbour down the road, would likely pitch in all he could, but he also had his farm, and wasn't as fit and active as he used to be.

"It's such a pity Joe isn't around," Seb sighed. Joe, Uncle Matt's previous farmhand, had got caught up with a gang of cattle rustlers earlier in the year. Seb had uncovered the identities of the men, but Joe had turned against his companions to help the young people when they ended up in danger. Joe had moved to Scotland for his own safety and wouldn't be back in Northern Ireland for a long time.

"Could we put an ad in the paper?" Seb began to clean the udders of the next batch of cows.

"Dad has tried that before. No one responded. People don't seem to want this sort of work, with irregular hours."

Seb bit his lip. This was Tuesday. School would be starting again on Monday. They had just under a week to find someone to help out. He would pray about it. Surely they would find someone by then.

"Matt's through his surgery." Aunt Karen set the portable phone on the kitchen table. She sounded weary and looked even worse. Her face was pale and dark circles stood out in sharp contrast under her eyes. She brushed a hand through her long brown hair and gave a small smile. "Everything went well."

"That's good, Aunt Karen," Seb responded. "How long will he be in hospital for?"

"About a week. Maybe a wee bit less."

"And how long until he's back to normal?" asked Lavinia.

Aunt Karen looked down, but not before Seb caught a troubled look in her eyes. "I don't know, Lavinia. I'm to meet the doctor tomorrow. We'll know then what his recovery is going to look like."

Seb didn't like the way his aunt was acting. Surely Uncle Matt would be okay. Did Aunt Karen think that he might never be the same again? If Uncle Matt couldn't work, what would become of Cherryhill Farm?

Aunt Karen lifted her head and tried to smile. "We'll go and see him later. He'll likely be pretty woozy with the anaesthetic, but I think it might do him good."

As they walked through the revolving doors of the hospital and down the corridor, the smells of antiseptic, toast and something unpleasant that Seb didn't want to think about too much assaulted his nostrils and awakened memories. He shuddered as the scenes from the evening he'd found Mum unconscious and beaten up in their living room passed through his mind. That night was still all too vivid in his memory and he tried to push it away. They were here to see Uncle Matt. Mum was safely at work in the nursing home and Dad was in prison on drug trafficking charges, where he couldn't hurt her now.

Aunt Karen pulled open a door that led to a stairwell and motioned Lavinia and Seb forward.

"Why don't we take the lift?" asked Lavinia.

An incredulous look was Aunt Karen's only response.

Lavinia gave Seb a quick grin. "Lifts are too slow for Mum," she whispered. "She only ever goes in one if it's over ten flights of stairs."

Seb hid a smile as Aunt Karen looked around. "Can't you two walk a little faster? You'd think you were twice my age."

They bustled after Aunt Karen as she made her way down a long corridor and hit a button on the wall to open a set of doors to their left. They'd barely opened before she squeezed through and began to walk down another corridor. Through the open doors lining the corridor, Seb caught glimpses of little rooms. Some sort of waiting room, with green chairs and a TV in the corner. A burst of laughter came from another room, and as Seb passed he caught sight of three nurses leaning against a bench with steaming mugs in their hands. Another room with a bed, an old, pale-faced man in paisley-print pyjamas reclining against the pillows, and a grey-haired lady pouring water from the blue-lidded water jug.

Aunt Karen stopped abruptly at the next door. Her hands smoothed her hair and she momentarily closed her eyes, then entered. Uncle Matt's room.

Seb's stomach fluttered. He wasn't sure what he expected to find. Would Uncle Matt look really sick? What would Seb say to him? Would Uncle Matt be mad at him for not preventing the bull from attacking him?

Lavinia followed her mum.

There was no time for further contemplation. Seb took a deep breath and stepped into the room.

Chapter Three

Lavinia gasped. "Is–is he okay?"

Seb peered over her shoulder at the person lying in the bed. Uncle Matt was pale and still.

At Lavinia's words, he stirred and his eyelids lifted slightly. "Vinnie?" he slurred.

"Dad!" Lavinia sprang to the bedside and knelt beside him, wrapping an arm around his chest.

"Careful, Lavinia," cautioned Aunt Karen. "Make sure you don't shake the bed or dislodge anything."

For the first time, Seb noticed a line coming from Uncle Matt's arm, leading to a clear fluid-filled bag on a stand beside the bed. Another tube protruded from beneath the bedclothes and led to another bag attached to the side of the bed. Seb shuddered. He really didn't like hospitals.

Lavinia pulled back and sat on the chair, grabbing her father's hand. "Are you okay?"

Uncle Matt looked up at her through squinted eyes. "Bit sore, but I'm fine." He turned his head slightly. "Seb?"

"Yes, I'm here, Uncle Matt."

A slight nod. "Thanks. Things might've been a lot worse."

"I'm sorry I didn't do more. I should have stopped the bull."

Uncle Matt gave a half laugh. "He was unstoppable."

Seb gave a wry grin. "He certainly was," he agreed.

"Dad, we've the TB–" Lavinia stopped abruptly at her mother's warning glare.

Uncle Matt blinked. "What were you going to say, Vinnie?"

"Oh, nothing. Just that we've got everything under control."

"That's good." His eyes drifted closed and Seb thought he'd gone back to sleep. They watched him in silence. It was startling to see big, strong Uncle Matt, the one they all depended on and relied on, lying weak and helpless in a hospital bed. His leg, the one that had been broken, was hidden by the bedclothes.

After long moments, Uncle Matt stirred again. "I'll be out of here soon. Then I'll get back to work."

Seb shot a look at Aunt Karen. She was frowning. "Now, Matt," she said mildly, "you'll need time to recover. You don't want to do any further damage."

"I'll be fine," he insisted. "But I think a good night's sleep would help. It's getting late; maybe you should head home. Turn off the lights on your way out, please."

Vinnie glanced at her watch, puzzlement showing on her face. "It's only three in the afternoon, Dad. It's still light outside."

"Huh?" He peered up at her.

"It's okay, Lavinia. I think it's time to go. I'll come back tomorrow." Aunt Karen bent over her husband and pressed a kiss to his lips, then smoothed his dark hair back from his forehead. "I love you," she said.

"Love you too, Karen."

Seb looked away awkwardly. His parents had never shown any affection to each other that he could recall and he wasn't used to it.

As they left the room, he glanced back at Uncle Matt. He looked so weak and groggy that Seb couldn't help but wonder if he would ever be well again. He tried to banish the thought from his mind as they made their way down the corridor. Of course he would recover.

Seb shivered as they exited the hospital and stepped into the late October afternoon.

They'd fixed Uncle Matt's leg. Very soon he'd be back to normal.

Wouldn't he?

"What are you doing?" Seb asked, walking into Uncle Matt's office after dinner. Lavinia was sitting at the computer, scrolling through a spreadsheet and frowning.

"It's the cows," she said. "I'm just checking when they're all due to calve."

Seb peered over her shoulder.

Lavinia pointed at the right hand column. "This is the approximate due date." She scrolled to the top. The first few cows had extra columns on the end of their rows, with the date of birth and gender of their calf. "These have all calved, and these," she pointed to the screen again, "have still to calve."

Seb winced. "That's a lot of cows."

"Mm-hm," Lavinia agreed. "And most of them are due to calve in the next six weeks. We really are going to have to get help."

"I wish we could think of someone," Seb said softly. "I've been praying about it."

Lavinia looked back at the screen and didn't speak. Seb wished that Lavinia knew the Lord Jesus Christ as her Saviour. Despite having been brought up hearing that she was a sinner needing to be saved, Lavinia still hadn't trusted Him. Did she know what she was missing out on? Seb couldn't understand it, but he would keep praying for her.

"So when is the next one due to calve?" he asked, turning his attention to the spreadsheet again.

Lavinia rubbed her brow. "The approximate date is Thursday, so that means she could go any day now. We'll have to keep an eye on her. Then there are another four due next week."

"Four?" Seb grimaced. They had school next week – his first week at his new school. He had only managed to keep up with the work during the first half of the term at his last school by sheer hard work and the help of his clever friend Edward, who had moved to Belfast from Malaysia. If Seb started to take days off now, he would fall badly behind. It would be a struggle to catch up and he might not get the grades he needed. Managing a large dairy farm, with milking, feeding, calving cows, and everything else that needed done, was tough enough, but adding school into the mix? How would they ever cope?

An old grey Landrover Defender pulled into the yard just after breakfast the next morning.

"It's Tommy," shouted Martha, pulling open the back door and waving frantically at the old neighbour as he made his way up the yard.

"Well, lass, how are you?" he said, patting the little girl's blonde head.

"Okay, Tommy," she answered, eyes bright. "How's Sweep?"

Tommy chuckled. "Still makin' Madge run in circles after him." He stepped into the kitchen.

"Oh dear," said Karen as she pulled another mug from the cupboard, poured in some milk, then filled it up with tea. "She'll be wanting a refund!"

"Ah! You know what my sister's like," he replied, blue eyes twinkling beneath his bushy grey brows. "She gives off plenty, but she doesn't mean the half o' it." He sat down and cupped rough, work-worn hands around his mug of tea. "What about Matt?" he asked, concern written in the lines of his face.

"He had his surgery yesterday," Karen replied. "It seemed to go well, but I hope to meet with the doctor later to get a few more details."

Tommy nodded slowly. "He'll be out o' action for a good wee while, I'm guessin'."

"I'd imagine so," Karen said.

"And I suppose a lot o' the cows are goin' to calve before Christmas."

"Most of them," Lavinia replied glumly. "This must be the very worst time for Dad to have an accident."

"I'm not sure anytime is a good time when you farm, lass."

"True," she replied. "It's a busy life."

Tommy lifted the mug to his mouth and took a sip. "Well, I might be an old man, but I'll do all I can to help. I can give a wee hand with the milkin' and anythin' else that's needin' done. With the calvin' too."

Karen smiled. "Thank you, Tommy. You know I appreciate that."

"Matt's done plenty for me over the years. At least the young'uns are off on holiday this week." He smiled across the table at Seb and Lavinia. "Won't be easy for a while, but you'll get by. I was enjoyin' a wee verse this morning. 'My God shall supply all your need according to His riches in glory by Christ Jesus.' "

"Thanks, Tommy." Aunt Karen smiled at the old farmer. Seb noticed a tear glint in her eye. She was trying to be strong, but this was an awful burden to be carrying around. It was a good reminder. God knew all about their need, even more than they did themselves. And He promised to supply it, to give what was needed to cope. He knew what was best.

"So what's the news around the country?" asked Lavinia, changing the subject. "Dad will want to know."

"Well, Madge was down at the shop the other day and heard that Freddy Robertson's son has got a buildin' site passed."

Lavinia's eyes widened. "He's getting married?"

Tommy chuckled. "That's what Madge asked, but apparently he's only gettin' it all prepared in case the right girl comes along."

"I don't know who'd want to marry him!" exclaimed Lavinia. "That moustache…" She shuddered.

"Now, Lavinia," her mother chided her. "Some girl somewhere will think that moustache is the best thing she's ever laid eyes on."

Lavinia spluttered with laughter. "Oh, Mum! Have you actually seen it? It's like something from the Boer War!"

Seb frowned. He'd have to search for 'Boer War Moustaches' on the internet later.

"The other piece of information," Tommy continued, his face grave, "is that a brave lot o' Henry Ramsey's cattle have tested positive for TB."

There was silence as the implications of Tommy's statement sunk in.

"Oh, Tommy!" groaned Lavinia. "Don't tell us that."

"Who's Henry Ramsey?" asked Seb.

"He owns a lot of land down the road a bit. In fact, a field of his borders ours." Lavinia looked worried.

"Does that put the cattle here at risk?" Seb asked.

Tommy sighed. "Son, most folk believe that badgers spread TB. You can't fence in badgers, so TB often spreads from farm to farm. Mind you, it doesn't always happen. I remember back a few years ago when Kieran Convery's cattle were infected, and yet not one o' his adjoinin' neighbours had even one inconclusive result."

"But it increases our risk," Seb said, dread forming in the pit of his stomach. Surely God wouldn't permit anything to happen to the cattle as well as what had happened to Uncle Matt. Surely He would preserve them from further trial. He had to! What would they do otherwise?

Chapter Four

"Seb, wake up!"

Seb felt as if he were trying to claw his way out of a deep pit. His eyes wouldn't open and he wanted nothing more than to pull the covers over his head and go back to sleep.

"*Seb!*" Louder this time.

He groaned. What on earth was wrong? Surely it wasn't the morning already.

"She's calving. I need your help!"

Calving! Seb emerged from his slumber like an express train bursting from a tunnel. They'd checked the heifer earlier and Lavinia had figured she was beginning to get ready to deliver a calf.

"Coming." He flung back the covers and leaped from his bed, then pulled on his jeans and sweatshirt, and raced downstairs to catch up with Lavinia. She was already back at the shed by the time he emerged from the house.

"What's wrong?" he asked as he entered the calving pen. The heifer was bellowing and huffing great puffs of air, arching her back.

Lavinia grimaced. "She should be further on than this. It's her first calf, though, so anything could happen."

"What should we do?"

"We need to secure her over there." She pointed to one side of the pen.

Seb opened the gate and stepped into the pen. The heifer's breath hovered as steam in the cold air of the frosty night. Seb guided the heifer to where his cousin had indicated. Lavinia pulled a gate across to form a small, cow-sized pen, and locked vertical head bars into position. She then fastened a chain between the wall and the gate, at the heifer's rear end. The heifer shuffled her feet and bellowed again.

Lavinia pushed up the sleeve of her sweatshirt as far as it would go, pulled on long plastic gloves and squeezed some lubricant gel onto the glove. She took a deep breath, then inserted her hand into the heifer's birth canal. After pushing her arm in until her cheek was almost resting against the heifer's flank, she felt around, a frown of concentration on her face.

"What can you feel?"

"Sh!" she hissed.

Seb impatiently rocked from foot to foot. Was the calf back to front? The head in the wrong position? The legs pointing backwards instead of forwards? Anything could be happening in there. Why wouldn't Lavinia tell him?

Finally, she pulled her arm out, dripping with blood and mucus. "The calf is in the right position, but... I don't know... it just seems big or something." She shrugged. "Maybe we'll give her another contraction or two, and if that doesn't work, we'll try the calving aid." She bit her lip nervously.

It was clear to Seb that Lavinia was feeling the strain of being in charge. Having only watched one calving before – and a straightforward one at that – he felt unknowledgeable and helpless. If only Uncle Matt was here.

They stood in silence as the heifer laboured through another contraction. Lavinia shook her head. "I'm going to get the calving aid. Nothing's happening."

As she disappeared out of the pen, Seb leaned back, one foot against the wall behind him. "Oh, God. Please… " His prayer whispered out in the exhale of his held breath. Cows were valuable, especially Uncle Matt's. And this was one of the best heifers. Her calf would also be worth a lot, especially with the good bloodlines.

Lavinia appeared from the gloom, hauling a long metal contraption behind her, and holding a bucket of disinfectant containing coloured ropes in her hand.

"Anything?" she asked hopefully.

Seb shook his head.

Lavinia rested the calving aid against the wall, set the bucket at Seb's feet and again reached her hand into the birth canal. "No further forward." She paused and looked in concern at the heifer. "And she's getting tired. I think we need to get this calf out. Right now."

"I'm sorry, Vinnie. I don't know how this works." Seb gestured to the calving aid.

"I've seen Dad do this. Hope I can remember." She held out her hand. "Give me the red rope."

Seb lifted the red rope out of the bucket and handed it to her. She slipped the loop over her hand, then inserted hand and rope into the canal. After a minute of working inside the heifer, she pulled her hand out. "Blue, please." She repeated the same process with the blue one. The two ropes now dangled from the opening.

"I need to get the ropes attached to the calving aid." She lifted the unwieldy contraption and rested the wide u-shaped end against the heifer's rump. She lifted the red rope. "It's red for right, but I can never remember if I'm supposed to attach the red rope to the calf's leg to *my* right, or to the *calf's* right leg."

"It probably doesn't matter, as long as you know which is which."

"Probably not." She attached the rope to the right side, and lifted the blue one.

"What do you want me to do?"

"I might need you to take your turn with this, but, in the meantime, be prepared to take this chain off and move the gate over. There's a good chance she'll fall."

At the next contraction, Lavinia worked the lever to ratchet the ropes tight.

"Anything?"

Lavinia shot Seb an impatient look. "You can see as well as I can."

The heifer began to strain again, and Lavinia worked as hard as she could. Two little white hooves appeared. With each contraction, more of the hooves appeared. Suddenly, the heifer leaned to her left. Seb struggled to release the chain. The instant the chain released, the labouring beast fell heavily to her side and the gate crashed back. Lavinia struggled to maintain her hold on the aid.

"I told you to let the gate out gently," she snapped.

"No–" Seb clamped his mouth shut. There was no point in arguing that she hadn't warned him that the heifer would slam down onto her side like that. Bickering wouldn't help the heifer, or alleviate Lavinia's worry. "Would you like me to take a turn?"

She shrugged. "Why not?"

Seb moved into the place Lavinia had vacated. "When do I pull?"

"When she strains… Like *now!*" The heifer strained and Seb worked the lever. The forelegs were beginning to appear.

"I need to check where the head is." Lavinia felt around inside and frowned. "It's there, but it's pointing up. I can't believe I missed that. Or maybe it was the… " She trailed off. "Was there another rope?"

Seb pointed to the bucket where he'd left it against the wall. Lavinia grabbed the rope from the bucket and draped it over her hand, before forcing it over the protruding legs into the inner cavity. She worked inside the heifer, her face contorting. She was almost lying flat on the ground, her clothes filthy.

Long moments later, she pulled her hand out. "Finally. Thank goodness for that cow calving video I watched online earlier." She attached the white rope and took over from Seb. "I got the head tilted down a bit and put the rope over each ear. When we pull this, it should bring the nose out in the right position."

Multiple contractions and ratcheting finally brought the head into view. Lavinia pulled the folds of the heifer's skin away from the calf's head.

"We're getting there," Seb said, wiping his brow. He no longer felt the chill of the late October night.

"It's taking too long," Lavinia replied. "I should have called the vet."

"Is it too late to call him now?"

The heifer arched her back and Lavinia worked the calving aid again. Finally, a black head popped out.

"That's the worst bit over." Lavinia didn't look in the slightest relieved. If anything, she looked even more worried.

Within minutes, the body slipped out, and Lavinia dropped the calving aid and swiftly pulled the ropes from the calf's head and legs. She began to furiously rub the little nose and body. There was no response.

"Help me out here, Seb," she said in a panicked voice.

"What do you want me to do?" The calf wasn't moving, but neither had the calf Seb had watched being born earlier in the autumn. He knelt down beside the little animal.

"Keep rubbing. I'm going to get cold water."

Seb began to rub the warm, wet body and nose. There was no response. Seb glanced at the heifer; she was still lying down.

Lavinia dashed back with a bucket of cold water. "Hold the head the right shape so I can get this water into its ear."

Seb looked up in puzzlement. "Its ear?"

"Yes, Seb!" Lavinia sounded exasperated. "And hurry!"

Seb held the head while Lavinia poured the water. Nothing. Not even a twitch.

"Oh, come on! Breathe!"

The last of the water washed into the black ear and overflowed. The calf remained as still as those Border Fine Arts ornaments in Uncle Matt and Aunt Karen's good sitting room. Lavinia caught the calf by the shoulders and shook. "Wake up!" The calf flopped over. Lavinia sank to her knees. Seb could see the hope draining from her like the water had drained from the bucket only a few minutes before. "It's dead." Her voice was muffled beneath her hands.

"Are you sure?"

Lavinia nodded. "It's my fault."

"Was it a boy or girl?"

"It doesn't matter. I don't think I want to know anyway."

"Your dad will want to know. And don't you need to register it even if it's... not living?" he finished.

Lavinia sighed, but pushed herself to her knees and checked anyway. "A heifer." Her voice cracked on the words. "And she's a beauty." She slammed her hand against her knee. "Stupid, stupid, stupid!"

Seb took a deep breath. Lavinia was starting to lose control, and the heifer was still on her side and looking listless. "Vinnie, do you think we'd need to do something with the mother?"

Lavinia glanced at the heifer. Her face crumpled and her shoulders shook. "I don't know that I can. I can't think what to do next, and she's too heavy to move, and I think we're going to lose her too."

Seb grabbed her by the arm and gave her a gentle shake. "Lavinia. We are *not* going to lose her. We can still help her. But you need to take a deep breath. Come on. Breathe in…" He waited until she took a shaky breath. "And out…and in…and out."

With a few breaths, Lavinia began to calm down. "Would you go and get Mum? She's always let Dad and me deal with all the farming stuff, but she had two babies herself. She might know what to do."

Seb ran back through the shed and across the yard. He kicked off his dirty boots at the back door and dashed up the stairs to Aunt Karen's bedroom.

"Aunt Karen?"

The door opened immediately. Aunt Karen stood in a blue dressing gown, looking wide awake. "Is everything okay?"

Seb shook his head. "The calf is dead, and the heifer's not doing well. Lavinia's doing even worse."

"Give me a minute." She disappeared back inside her room and shut the door. Seb went downstairs and worked his wellies on again. As he straightened, he heard the door close softly behind him.

"Was the calf in the wrong position?" Aunt Karen asked as they walked across the yard.

"No. At least not initially. She was just too big and it took too long."

"She." A look of sadness washed over Aunt Karen's face. "Matt hoped this one would be a heifer. He'd high hopes for her." She sighed. "Why didn't you come for me sooner?"

"I don't know. I guess we were too busy to properly consider it."

"I don't think I'd have been able to save her life anyway," Aunt Karen replied. "Seb." She stopped just outside the shed and touched his arm. "I know you've been praying, and I know you're likely thinking that God isn't listening tonight."

Seb winced guiltily. The thought had gone through his head.

"God always has a reason for how He answers our prayers. Because the calf died, it doesn't mean the mother will die too. So let's pray. Lavinia needs all the prayer she can get right now."

Aunt Karen and Seb closed their eyes, and right there, in the frosty night, outside the shed door, Aunt Karen beseeched God for wisdom for her daughter, for the recovery of the sick heifer and, most surprising of all to Seb, that God would be glorified in the sad events of this dark October night.

Chapter Five

Uncle Matt's jeep, driven by Aunt Karen, pulled to a stop in the yard. Seb, Lavinia and Martha, who was hopping excitedly from foot to foot, waited on the step, while the passenger door opened, and a pair of grey metal crutches emerged, then legs, and finally Uncle Matt.

Martha leaped off the step and flung herself at her daddy.

"Whoa, princess!" chuckled Matt, grabbing the door of the jeep. "I'm not used to balancing on three legs yet."

Martha pulled back to stare at his legs, then gazed up at him. "They gave you an extra leg? To make up for the one that's broken?"

Lavinia giggled at the look of puzzlement on the little girl's face.

"No, sweetheart." Aunt Karen was pulling the overnight bag from the back of the jeep. "Daddy means his good leg, and the two crutches. He still has two legs, but he's not allowed to put any weight on the broken one. The crutches help him balance, but he needs some practice."

Uncle Matt adjusted the crutches under his arms, then hopped a little unsteadily to the step. He paused and frowned.

"Come on, Daddy! You can do it!" Martha said.

Matt reached forwards and placed the crutches on the lower step, then hopped. He wobbled, then began to topple backwards. Aunt Karen flung the bag aside and braced her petite frame against his back. Seb reached for his arm, and between them they managed to steady him.

"Thanks." Uncle Matt grinned, but Seb could see a flicker of pain, and something else that he couldn't quite identify, in his eyes.

They helped him up the remaining step and into the house, seated him in the comfy armchair by the fire, and tripped over each other to be the first to get him a cup of tea and the tin of gypsy creams that Madge had sent over.

After the fuss had died down and everyone was sitting with their own choice of beverage and the tin of chocolate-sandwiched biscuits on the coffee table, Uncle Matt looked around at them all with a smile. "It's good to be home."

Lavinia smiled back. "I'm really glad you're home too." She looked exhausted.

"How have things been going?" Matt asked, his face serious.

Lavinia opened her mouth, then closed it.

"Come on, Vinnie. Tell me. I might have broken my leg, but there's nothing wrong with my brain. Well," he grinned, "not that they told me."

Lavinia took a breath. "The heifer calved. The calf was dead."

Uncle Matt's face fell. "Bull or heifer?"

"Heifer. She was really big. I'm sorry, Dad. I should have called the vet."

Matt gave a slight frown, but took a sip of tea. "Things happen, Vinnie. Don't beat yourself up about it. I've delivered dead calves before too. Is the heifer okay?"

"She's totally fine now. She wasn't too good afterwards, though. We gave her a drink of that stuff that the feed rep recommended to perk her up."

"How many to calf next week? Three?"

"Four."

Matt nodded. "We'll manage." But he looked worried. "And the bull?"

"He's still there. I wasn't sure what to do with him."

"He'll be destroyed. I'll make a few phone calls and get that sorted."

"Um, Dad?"

"What is it, Vinnie?"

"The TB test… "

Uncle Matt hit the heel of his hand against the arm of the chair and groaned. "I'd forgotten all about that. It's Tuesday, isn't it?"

Lavinia nodded. "We can take the day off school."

Aunt Karen immediately shook her head. "Oh, no, Lavinia. I don't think that's a good idea, especially for Seb. It'll only be his second day at his new school."

"Well, *I* can take the day off, then."

Uncle Matt looked at Aunt Karen. "Actually, Karen, I don't think we have an option. I need them here. If we move the first visit to Wednesday, then they can do the readings on Saturday when Seb and Vinnie are off school." He turned to his older daughter. "What time is the test?"

"I think it's around ten. Let me check." She hopped off the seat and disappeared through the door to the office. "Ten thirty," she yelled.

"Bring me the phone, please," Matt called back.

Lavinia handed the phone to him and waited while he called.

"Hello, Kate, it's Matt McRoss here... Oh, not so bad, home today... Yes, a bit sore, but I'll live... Yes... Uh-huh... Yes... Uh, I was wondering... What's that? Oh, yes, she's been doing a great job..." Matt rolled his eyes while the voice on the other end of the phone chattered on. Finally, he was able to speak. "Who's scheduled to do the test on Tuesday, do you know?... Ah, that's great... Well, I was wondering if there was any chance that we could... Is that right now? Fancy that! Kate, is there any chance of Diarmuid coming on Wednesday instead, and a wee bit later, maybe just after lunch? It's just that these young ones will need to be here to help and they're back to school next week... What's that?... No, not Martha. I'm talking about Lavinia and my nephew... Yes, he's back. He and his mum moved from Belfast, but he's been staying here since my accident... Yes, that's the one..." Matt sighed. "Kate, could you ask Diarmuid and get back to me?...

Okay, that's good. Thanks, Kate... Yes, I'll tell her... No problem at all... Right, bye!"

Matt ended the call and flung the phone onto the coffee table. It slid along and crashed into the tin of biscuits. Aunt Karen grabbed it before it went flying.

"That *woman!*" he exclaimed. "I don't know why they keep her on. She does nothing but talk!"

"Matt!" scolded Karen. "She's a very nice lady, even if she does have a little problem with excessive chattiness."

"Huh! Little?!" grumbled Matt, but he straightened up and grinned at Seb and Lavinia. "Hopefully she'll not forget to ask Diarmuid."

"Aw, I'm glad it's Diarmuid," said Lavinia. "He's really nice. He's from County Kerry and he has the most *amazing* accent."

Seb chuckled. "Watch out, Caleb," he mumbled, then hastily slid away from the elbow aimed at his ribs.

"Don't be stupid, Seb. All I said was–"

"Vinnie," Matt warned.

Lavinia glared at Seb, then turned her back to him. "Dad, did you hear that some of Henry Ramsey's cattle tested positive for TB?"

Uncle Matt froze. "Where did you hear that?" His voice was low and earnest.

"Tommy."

Matt briefly closed his eyes and shook his head. "That's not good."

"What's not good, Daddy?" Martha came to sit on the arm of his chair.

He put an arm around her and smiled at her. "Nothing you need to worry about, princess."

"Are the cows sick?"

"The cows? No, they aren't sick."

"But Henry's cows. Are they sick?"

"Not really, Martha."

The little face still looked troubled. Martha was such a kind little soul. She hated to see anything suffering.

"Why don't you go and get Glen and show me how big he's got."

Her eyes widened. "Bring him into the house again?" She shot a glance at her mother.

Karen rolled her eyes. "Just this once. The poor dog hardly knows whether he's allowed inside or not these days."

Martha raced through the kitchen and out the back door.

"Vinnie, about the TB test, there's nothing we can do. Pray and wait. As my granny used to say, let's not meet trouble halfway."

Lavinia nodded, then glanced at her watch. "I guess it's time to milk." She stood up and lifted the mugs from the coffee table.

Seb stood as well.

"I wish I could be out there too."

"I know, Uncle Matt. But don't worry, we're managing okay."

Uncle Matt looked like he wanted to say something, but "thank you" was all he said.

Seb reached for his Bible and notebook on the bedside table, then rummaged around for a pen. He was sure he'd left it right beside his Bible, but it wasn't there now. He dropped to the floor and peered underneath the bed. Nothing. Well, it didn't matter. There were always plenty of pens in this house from all sorts of companies, advertising all sorts of things – animal feeds, fertilisers, pharmaceuticals, tractors. It would take less time to run downstairs and grab one than it would to keep searching.

He pulled open the door and padded down the hall and stairs in his socks. As he approached the living room door, he could hear voices. He paused. Uncle Matt and Aunt Karen were having a discussion. He had raised his hand to lightly knock the door when he heard Uncle Matt speak.

"Karen, there's no way those kids can run a farm, never mind the fact that they need to go to school. It just won't work."

"Well, maybe we can find someone."

Seb heard a sigh. "We've been through this before. When Joe had to leave I asked everyone I could think of. No one can help, and nobody knows anyone who can."

"That was in the summer. Maybe now that the silaging season is over, someone will be free." Aunt Karen's voice was soothing.

Seb heard a clatter and jumped. Uncle Matt growled. "Stupid crutches! I hate being like an invalid. Can't even move around by myself. You had to catch me earlier. You, all five foot of you, had to catch *me*!"

"Oh, come on, Matt! I'm a bit taller than five foot." Aunt Karen sounded artificially cheery.

"That's not the point," he continued. "The point is that I'm supposed to be looking after you and the girls, and Seb, and instead everyone has to run around after me, and I can't even run my own farm." His voice cracked. "If I can't do that, what use am I anyway?"

Seb spun around. He'd heard more than he wanted to. He crept slowly up the stairs and fell at the side of his bed. He felt sick. Seb had never seen Uncle Matt cross, not even when Seb crashed his pickup the day he'd arrived at Cherryhill. And now he was angry, frustrated and broken. And it was all Seb's fault.

"God, *why* did that bull have to attack? Why Uncle Matt? Why not me?" Angry tears began to stream down his face. He dashed them away with the cuff of his sweatshirt. What if more cows had trouble calving? What if the TB test came back positive? What if Uncle Matt's injuries never really healed properly? What if the farm couldn't sustain itself under him and Lavinia? What if…

He tried to dispel his worries, and lifted his Bible. Even if he couldn't make notes, he could still read. As Seb flicked through the pages to find tonight's chapter in the book of Acts, an underlined verse in Philippians caught his eye, and his hand stilled.

Be anxious for nothing, but in everything by prayer and supplication, with thanksgiving, let your requests be made known to God; and the peace of God, which surpasses all understanding, will guard your hearts and minds through Christ Jesus.

Peace. Exactly what everyone needed right now.

Chapter Six

"Seb, I brought your new blazer." Mum smiled at him across the kitchen table, a forkful of roast beef and gravy halfway to her mouth.

"Oh, Julie!" Aunt Karen gave a little chuckle. "I'd forgotten all about Seb needing a new uniform. I would have helped you work out what new clothes he needed."

"I know you would," Mum replied, "but the man in the shop was very helpful. I didn't want to trouble you; you've plenty to keep you busy right now."

"It's okay if I stay on here at Cherryhill, isn't it?" asked Seb. He missed Mum but he hoped she hadn't decided that it was time he moved back home. After all, the plan had been that he and Mum would live in the little bungalow on the outskirts of town, and Seb would visit the farm, not move there to live.

"Oh, of course it is, Seb," Mum said. "I know how much you're needed here for now." She was being very generous. He knew how much she'd been looking forward to them living in their new house.

Uncle Matt cleared his throat. "I'm sorry about this, Julie. I'm going to start looking for help tomorrow."

"Just you concentrate on getting better, Matt. I'm glad Seb is useful to you. You've both done so much for us that it'll only go a short distance in repaying you."

"No need to repay us, Julie. You're family." Matt gave his wife's sister a warm smile. Seb's mum hadn't always been so fond of her family, having rejected it and run away from home when she was only seventeen. God's salvation had made a remarkable change in Mum's life. Now Dad was the only dark spot in the bright new vista.

"Apart from the blazer and part of the PE kit, I think most of the uniform is the same anyway," Mum continued. "It's great that the trousers and shirts are the same colour as the uniform for Seb's last school. That's saved us having to buy a whole new uniform after only two months."

Only two months. Sometimes Seb couldn't get over the speed with which his life had changed. It was unbelievable that in the not-too-distant past he'd been a rebel, a troubled teen who hated his life and nearly everyone in it. Nowadays, he was a child in God's family, enjoying life and a peace that he'd never known existed.

And now he was changing schools. He hadn't had time to think about it over the past week, but it was real. Tomorrow morning, he'd put on his new blazer, pick up his schoolbag, which was empty again, and catch the bus with Lavinia to the school gates.

"Are you nervous, Seb?" asked Aunt Karen sympathetically.

"A little," he admitted. "But at least I know Vinnie."

"And Rebekah," Lavinia added, a mischievous smirk on her face.

"Rebekah?" asked Mum. "Oh, the pretty blonde girl I met this morning at church? The Harveys' daughter?"

"Yep, that's her, Aunt Julie!" replied Lavinia. "What did you think of her?"

"She seems to be a lovely girl. Very friendly."

Lavinia grinned. "Seb thinks so too."

Seb narrowed his eyes at his cousin. She was sitting too far away for him to kick her under the table, and she gave him a smug look. He opened his mouth to rib her about Caleb, then thought better of it. Lavinia didn't enjoy being teased as much as she enjoyed teasing others, and the last thing Seb needed was for her to be in a huff when he was depending on her tomorrow. If Lavinia wasn't speaking to him, dear knows where he'd end up in a strange school building.

Seb was looking forward to a fresh start. At his last school, his reputation as a troublemaker was cemented in the minds of the teachers. Even though he'd changed when he'd trusted Christ, had become a new creation, as the Bible said, the teachers hadn't quite believed that the change was permanent. At this school, no one really knew about his previous actions, and he was glad for the opportunity to make good first impressions.

After dinner, Aunt Karen and Mum shooed everyone away from the table as they began to clear up. Seb took himself to his bedroom. He'd been so tired this week after working each day on the farm, and he wanted to catch up on his Bible study. He lifted his Bible, notebook, pen and special highlighters for marking Bible pages, and opened it at the book of Acts, chapter eight. There were things in the first half of the chapter that he didn't really understand, so he had lots of questions written down to ask Uncle Matt when he got the chance. Had Simon the sorcerer really believed? Or was the man only pretending? *He wouldn't have been the first person ever to do that*, Seb thought wryly.

Today, however, he was going to look at the next part of the chapter, about a preacher called Philip and a man from Ethiopia. Seb stretched out on his side on the bed and began to read. The Ethiopian man had been to Jerusalem and was reading in the book of Isaiah on his return journey. He wasn't understanding it very well, so Philip stopped the chariot, climbed up beside him and explained the passage to him, preaching Jesus.

Next thing, the man was asking for baptism. Seb sat up. "Huh? What's going on here?"

He read on. 'Then Philip said, "If you believe with all your heart, you may." And he answered and said, "I believe that Jesus Christ is the Son of God." '

Seb set his Bible on his knees. There was no doubt the man had trusted Christ, likely when Philip was speaking to him. But what was all this about baptism? This wasn't the first time Seb had come across this word. He'd heard people talking about baptism, but he had thought it had something to do with babies, and wasn't something that grown men did. He'd never seen one. Why did people do it? Was it optional? Surely it wasn't necessary for salvation? He uncapped the pen and opened the notebook to a clean page. 'Research baptism' he scribbled. Maybe he could ask Uncle Matt for pointers on studying this new topic.

He continued reading for a while, highlighting key words and jotting down notes as he went on.

"Seb?" Mum's voice drifted up the stairs.

"Coming!" Seb stretched. He closed his Bible and notebook and set them on the bedside table, then raced down the stairs. Mum was waiting at the bottom.

"I thought we could go for a walk. It's crazy, but I've hardly got talking to you at all since we moved from Belfast."

Seb grinned. "Things didn't work out the way we'd planned."

Mum raised her eyebrows. "They certainly did not! But we know that God has a good reason for this, even if we don't know what it is."

Seb rubbed his toe on the carpet. God might have a good reason, but Seb hated seeing a good family suffering.

"So will we go for that walk?" Mum gave his arm a gentle squeeze.

Seb nodded and made his way through the living area and kitchen to the back door, where he pulled on his boots. He backtracked into the office and lifted Glen's lead, then joined Mum at the door.

"Nice wellies."

"Thanks!" She chuckled. "Thankfully Karen and I have the same size of feet. Wellies do feel strange though, after so many years."

Seb clipped the lead to Glen's collar and they made their way down the back lane. Jess trotted along behind, pausing to sniff the bushes now and again.

"I'm wondering about withdrawing the complaint against your dad."

Seb missed a step and nearly fell. "You're what?" he asked, after he regained his balance. Why would Mum do that? The man had given her years of grief and finally tried to kill her. "Don't you think he should face justice?"

She looked at Seb sadly. "To have to testify and relive it all over again... I don't know if I can do that." She gazed at a spot on the horizon. "You know, I don't know if God is changing my heart towards him, but I sort of feel sorry for him. His trial for drug trafficking is coming up soon, and since Gran died, he really has no one. You and I are his only family."

"He doesn't deserve a family!" Seb exclaimed. "Not after how he treated us."

"Seb, you know that none of us deserve anything. God gives us things because He is gracious, not because we earn it. But, leaving that aside, your dad is loved by God. He gave His Son so that even your dad could be saved."

"I know that," Seb admitted, "but I can't imagine Dad believing there is a God, let alone trusting Christ."

"I have to admit that it's hard to envisage," Mum replied. "Nevertheless, I'm praying that God will help me to forgive him for how he's treated me over the years."

Seb looked up in alarm. "Oh, Mum! Please don't tell me you'd actually take him back?"

Mum's steps slowed and she stopped, a sad and distant look in her eyes. "This isn't how I imagined my life would turn out. Seb, even if I have forgiven him, it doesn't change the fact that I wouldn't feel at all safe with him in the house. And yet..."

Seb clenched his teeth. He couldn't understand the power that Dad had over Mum, even after he'd beaten her up so badly that Seb had thought she was dead, and even after Mum was delivered from the dark shadows that seemed to chase her from morning to night.

"I..." Mum paused and caught her lip between her teeth.

"What is it?" Surely she hadn't actually phoned up the prison and talked to Dad?

"Oh, don't worry. Let's talk about something else."

"Mum, just say it!" Seb burst out, frustrated.

She took a breath. "Dad has requested a visit from me."

Seb immediately shook his head. "No, Mum. Absolutely not. Seeing him again would only set you back. You need time and space."

She nodded slowly. "That's what I thought too."

"And how did he get in touch? Surely he doesn't know where we live?" Dad might be in prison, but Seb sincerely hoped that he didn't know where their new house was.

"He supplied our old address to the staff who organise the visits, but because I had mail redirection set up, the letter came to our new house."

Seb relaxed and took a breath.

"He also requested a visit from you."

Seb froze. He could feel goosebumps rising on his arms. Dad wanted a visit from him? "Why?"

Mum shrugged. "I don't know. He's probably lonely. I can't imagine any of his friends would make the effort to go and visit."

Seb shuddered. He'd thought about visiting Dad. Once, way back when he and Mum first moved from Belfast. It had seemed like a good and noble idea at the time. But now, when he was faced with the opportunity? It was the last thing he wanted to do. How could he willingly go and sit and talk to the man who had ruined so much of his life? The father that seemed to wish he'd never existed? The one who held his son in such disdain that he delighted in mocking him, and even tried to get him into trouble with the law?

"I couldn't, Mum." Seb was trembling. Whether from anger or fear, or a mix of old emotions rolled into one, he wasn't sure. All he knew was that even thinking of his father produced a reaction similar to that of a horrific nightmare.

He flinched when a hand touched his arm.

"I'm sorry, Seb. I shouldn't have mentioned it. You've suffered a lot from him too. Let's not worry about it."

Seb took a breath. "It's okay, Mum. Maybe someday I'll be able to see him again. But not right now."

Would he ever be able to face his father again? Seb glanced across the green fields. It didn't seem possible. In fact, right now, he really wouldn't mind if he never saw the man again. Ever.

Chapter Seven

"Lavinia! If you don't get a move on this minute, you're going to miss the bus!" Aunt Karen hollered up the stairs. Seb forced himself to swallow another spoonful of porridge and glanced at the clock. Usually Aunt Karen's meals were so delicious that he had to have seconds, but today his stomach was in knots. He couldn't remember when he'd last felt so nervous.

Lavinia bounded down the stairs and raced into the kitchen. She was carrying her school bag in one hand and her shoes in the other. Her school tie was draped around her neck and her blazer was over her arm. Aunt Karen shook her head. "Lavinia, you aren't even properly dressed!"

"It's okay, Mum. The bus is never early." She dropped her shoes to the floor and shoved her feet into them as she reached for the bowl of porridge.

Uncle Matt looked at Seb and winked. "Takes after her mother, that one! Always dashing around at the last minute, trying to do three things at once."

Aunt Karen whirled round. "Matt McRoss! You're the reason I have to do three things at once. There aren't many men who need as much looking after as you do! And I'm talking about before your accident."

Uncle Matt grinned at Seb and reached for the Bible which was sitting beside his bowl. "Seb, make sure you get a wife as good as your Aunt Karen." He flicked through the pages. "Vinnie, you may eat and listen at the same time."

Lavinia groaned. "Dad, we're really rushing here. Can't we leave it until later?"

Matt shook his head. "You know that's not the way it works, Vinnie. We work our lives around God's word, not the other way round. I know it's a really busy time for you and Seb, but we'll have to be more organised."

Uncle Matt read a short passage from the book of Proverbs and then prayed. He'd barely said 'amen' when Lavinia leaped from her seat and grabbed her bag. "Come on, Seb."

Seb pushed back his chair and lifted his own school bag. Lavinia was already outside, rounding the corner of the house and dashing down the lane towards the road.

"Have a good day!" called Aunt Karen.

"Thanks!" Seb sprinted to catch up with his cousin.

"Honestly," she grumbled, "we rushed like crazy to get through the milking and feeding, got ready for school and took a minute or two to grab breakfast, and Dad decides that we have all the time in the world for reading and praying!"

Seb frowned. Lavinia had never complained about the family's morning Bible reading before. "Well, have we missed the bus?" he asked.

"Who knows? This is the time it comes, so if it was early..." She trailed off and tilted her head to the side. "I think I hear it. Quick!" She broke into a trot, her bag bouncing on her back. As they reached the bottom of the lane, the bus pulled into view and slowed. Looking both ways, they crossed the road, then boarded the bus.

Seb stopped at the top of the steps and began to fumble in his blazer pocket for the change Aunt Karen had given him for the bus fare. The driver looked at him strangely. "Are you paying?"

"Yes. I don't live here, so I don't have a bus pass."

The driver shrugged, took the money and gestured to the ticket which had emerged from the machine. Seb pulled it free, then began to walk down the aisle, searching for Lavinia. The bus set off with a jolt and Seb grabbed the nearest bar.

"Seb!" Lavinia stood up and waved. "Down here!"

Seb staggered to the back of the bus. Each bump and corner seemed to conspire to knock him off balance, but finally he sank into the seat which his cousin indicated.

"Everybody, this is my cousin, Seb," Lavinia announced.

Seb glanced around at the curious faces and smiled politely. "Hi."

"Are you from Belfast?" A freckled-faced boy in front of Seb turned around and sneered.

Uh-oh. Obviously being from Belfast wasn't a desirable quality in this area. He nodded, but before he got a chance to elaborate, Lavinia butted in. "Carl, he might be from Belfast, but he's more of a farmer than you are. He can drive tractors, milk and calve cows as good as me. Better than you."

"Huh! That's impossible. What do townies know about farming?" The bus slowed and stopped to pick up another passenger.

Lavinia shot the boy a withering look and turned away. "Ignore him, Seb. He's a wee know-it-all."

"I am not!" Carl screeched. "I don't know why you–" He broke off as a large hand clamped down on his shoulder. A tall, broad-shouldered teen, who looked to be Seb's age, blocked the aisle.

"What're you spouting off about now, kid?"

The boy glared at the intruder but kept quiet. The giant threw his schoolbag into the overhead rack and slid into the back corner of the bus.

"So is this your famous cousin, Vin?"

"Yep, this is Seb. And don't call me that, *Dan*!"

The teen's eyes crinkled and he lifted a hand in greeting. "Hi, Seb! You're quite the legend, you know."

Seb blinked. "Am I?"

"Vin talks non-stop about you. According to her, you singlehandedly put down a whole gang of cattle rustlers, busted a big drug-smuggling operation and rescued someone from a burning building that was on the point of collapse. Not to mention being a natural-born farmer."

Seb glanced at Lavinia, who was suddenly preoccupied with her nails. "It really wasn't that big a deal," he said.

The bus slowed and stopped again. Seb looked up to see Rebekah and some of her siblings board the bus. She sat down beside Lavinia in the seat across the aisle from Seb, and gave him a warm smile. "Hi. Good to see you here, Seb."

Seb grinned back at his friend. It was great to see a familiar face. Rebekah had been with Seb when they were tied up in a dirty shed by the cattle rustlers, and she'd been quoting a verse from the Bible when Seb put his trust in the Lord Jesus Christ. He knew that there would always be a bond between them because of that.

"Hey!" A loud voice came from the back seat. "You never said hello to me!"

Rebekah swivelled around. "Sorry, Danny! Hello to you!" She laughed, then turned back and began to chat with Lavinia.

Seb glanced back at Danny. He had the appearance of a huge St Bernard dog who was being ignored. He frowned. Lavinia had said that Rebekah was popular. Did every male in her class fight for her attention? He'd have to be careful not to make enemies… or become jealous himself. He had no claim on Rebekah. He wasn't even wanting a girlfriend yet. Not for a few years at least. He had too much to do. He was determined to work hard, to make something of himself. To become an honest, decent, hardworking man, one who could support a wife and maybe even children. Someone the complete opposite of his dad. He swallowed. Why did he even have to think about him today of all days? Seb was mostly able to forget about him, but he was still there, haunting the dark corners of his mind. He'd really rather just put him out of his head. But why would Mum even suggest that he visit him?

The bus slowed to turn right at a junction on the outskirts of town. They weren't far from the school. Seb tried to block all thoughts of Dad from his mind. There was enough to worry about right now.

———

"Come and get cookies!" Martha met them at the door that afternoon, bouncing up and down in her pink sock soles. "Mummy made them special for you cause she says that you have lots of work to do and need… " She frowned and twisted her little mouth to one side in concentration. "Energy!" she finished triumphantly.

"What kind of cookies?" Lavinia asked her baby sister.

"Chocolatey cookies. The brown ones."

"Triple chocolate?" Lavinia's eyes lit up and she threw her schoolbag through the open office doorway before making her way into the kitchen.

Aunt Karen was pouring mugs of milk. Sure enough, a plate of cookies was ready and waiting on the table. "Hi, Seb, Lavinia. How was school?"

Lavinia sighed. "Boring as usual."

Uncle Matt was in the armchair beside the fire, one leg propped up on a fabric-covered footstool. He twisted around to look at them. "How did you find it, Seb?"

"It was okay. I think I've a bit of catching up to do. They're further ahead in this year's curriculum than we were at my last school."

"And how did you find the pupils? Did they give you any bother?"

Seb shrugged. "Not really. I got called 'townie' a few times by some of the farmers, but Vinnie put them straight."

"We're doing a good job of getting rid of that Belfast accent, don't you think, Dad?"

Uncle Matt laughed. "I wonder what the Belfast people would think of yours, Vinnie? They'd probably think you sound like Madge!"

"Really?" Lavinia looked aghast.

Aunt Karen pushed the mugs across the table. "If you two have your hands washed, sit down and get your cookies. Don't forget you've the milking to do."

Lavinia pulled out a seat and reached for a cookie. "Dad, that reminds me," she called over her shoulder. "I was talking to Danny Carson today. He's offered to lend a hand if we need help with the TB test and things like that."

"Is that Stevie's son?"

"Yes, that's him. I can give you his number and you can talk to him if you want."

"Thanks, Vinnie. An extra pair of hands could come in handy." He took a sip of tea, then set it on a small table at his elbow. "Tommy was around earlier. He's insisting on helping out. He was wanting to do all the milking, but I put my foot down. He's an old man, and he's his own farm to run. We came to an agreement that he'll help with the milking a couple of evenings a week, and help with the farm work when he has some time he can spare during the mornings."

"Hopefully that'll mean you'll get more time for your homework," Aunt Karen said, breaking a cookie in half and taking a dainty bite.

"Homework is such a waste of time," Lavinia grumbled.

"Now, Lavinia!" her mother scolded. "I don't want you leaving school with hardly a qualification to your name. You might think that farming is all you'll ever do, but it's a whole lot easier passing those exams in your teens than it is when things maybe don't work out the way you've planned."

"Did you ask the teacher about getting out for the TB test?" Matt asked.

"Yes," replied Lavinia. "She frowned and complained a bit, but when I explained what had happened she was all concerned and said that was fine. It's okay for Seb to get out too as long as we bring a note."

"I'm sure she wasn't too happy with you getting out early during your first week," Aunt Karen said.

Seb shrugged. “She didn’t say much about that, just that I have to make sure I catch up on the work so I don’t fall too far behind.” Right now, though, he wasn’t sure how he’d manage to keep up with the work at all. He was already beginning to feel exhausted from his early morning and busy day. How he’d be able to manage until bedtime, never mind until the weekend, he didn’t really know.

Chapter Eight

"I'm so glad that Dad got Freddy to come and get rid of that bull yesterday," Lavinia called to Seb. All the dairy cows were penned in the yard, waiting for the first part of their TB test, and the noise was akin to that in a department store on the first day of the January sales.

Seb nodded in agreement. He wasn't sorry when he'd noticed the empty pen yesterday at milking time. An animal that unpredictable could have been a potential disaster on a day like today.

A red pickup truck pulled into the yard. "Oh, good. There's Diarmuid. Now we can get started."

Seb watched as the truck door swung open and a well-built young man emerged. He donned a pair of plastic trousers and wellies, then strapped a belt around his waist. Inserting injectors into each holster, he made his way towards them.

"Well, Vinnie," he called in a thick Southern Irish brogue. "It's this time again."

Lavinia smiled at the dark-haired man. "Badly timed," she replied. "Dad's going crazy inside. Mum won't let him come out because he needs to be sitting with his leg up."

The vet nodded in concern. “An awful thing to happen, Vinnie. Awful. It could have been much worse, of course. But, still, an awful thing.” He turned around to greet Seb and his bright blue eyes crinkled shut. “And you must be the nephew Matt talked about.”

“Yes, I’m Seb.”

“Pleased to meet you, Seb.” He turned back to Vinnie. “Well, Vinnie, let’s get started.”

Lavinia led the way to the cattle crush and opened the bar to let the first cow enter. Diarmuid trimmed the hair in two places with a small pair of scissors, then measured each site with a pair of callipers. After injecting the tuberculin into the cow’s neck from the injector from the right hand holster, he repeated the same process at the lower site, using tuberculin from the left hand holster. “Avian tuberculin and bovine tuberculin,” Diarmuid replied, when Seb asked what the difference was. “It helps us to compare the reaction.”

Lavinia opened the bars at the front and the cow exited the crush. After slamming them shut, she opened the back bar, ready for the next cow. Seb steered another cow in, and the process began all over again.

Diarmuid kept up a steady conversation with Lavinia while he worked. Seb had thought they’d switch roles after a while, but Lavinia seemed glued to the young vet’s side. He hadn’t known that his cousin had such an interest in Gaelic football, or was so keen to hear how close Kerry, Diarmuid’s county’s team, had come to winning the Sam

Maguire Cup this year.

Even though Diarmuid was working at a steady pace, there were still plenty more cows to be tested. The plan was to get through most of the milking cows before it was time for the afternoon milking.

"How's it going, Seb?" A voice came from the far side of the yard. Seb glanced across to see Uncle Matt on crutches, leaning on the bar of the gate.

"Uncle Matt! Does Aunt Karen know you're out here?"

Matt chuckled wryly. "She gave me a permit for ten minutes. If I overstay, she said she'll come out and bodily carry me back to the house."

Seb laughed at the mental image of tiny Aunt Karen hefting big, solid Uncle Matt over her shoulder. "I think you're safe enough."

"Looks like Diarmuid is getting through them rightly." Uncle Matt indicated towards the cattle crush.

Seb nodded. "He's not wasting any time. We're getting there."

"That young fellow Danny Carson is coming to help after school, and I just phoned Caleb there to see if he'd help one of you with this evening's milking."

Seb hid a grin. He could see trouble ahead.

"Tommy was really annoyed that his hospital appointment was this afternoon. He said he'd cancel it, but Madge nearly had a fit. He's waited about a year for this appointment." He grimaced.

"Is your leg hurting you?" Seb asked.

"What? Oh. Yes, a wee bit, I guess." But a shadow passed across Uncle Matt's face that filled Seb with a sense of foreboding. This was nothing to do with physical pain.

Despite his upbeat attitude, Uncle Matt was worried about this TB test.

As Seb herded a cow towards the crush, he heard the sound of a car pulling into the yard. Minutes later, both Caleb and Danny appeared in the shed. Uncle Matt must have asked Caleb to collect Danny.

"How goes it?" the tall, redheaded young man asked.

Seb slapped the cow's rump to encourage her into the crush, then turned around.

"Not too bad, Caleb. Still got a lot to do, but we can make a start on the milking and Diarmuid will keep working."

"Do you want me to take over from you or Vinnie?" Danny asked.

Seb smirked. "Want to ask her?"

He could tell that Lavinia hadn't even noticed that anyone else was in the shed. Over the course of the afternoon, the conversation had moved from Gaelic football, to an in-depth discussion of the best brand of ketchup, Lavinia's woes with schoolwork, the worst veterinary cases Diarmuid had ever seen, and currently the topic of conversation seemed to be a detailed debate about facial hair, prompted, Seb guessed, by talk of Freddy Robertson Jr's new moustache.

Seb looked at Caleb. He was standing, feet apart, eyes narrowed, face slightly flushed. A quick glance confirmed what Seb had thought. He actually had his fists clenched.

"Vinnie," Seb called, before Caleb had a chance to react.

Lavinia looked up. "Oh, hi, Caleb," she said, a little too brightly. "And Danny? What are you doing here?"

"Your dad phoned me earlier."

"He never said. I guess we were so busy, he likely didn't get a chance."

"So who's helping me with the milking?" asked Caleb, looking hopefully towards Lavinia.

She immediately dropped her head and kicked a clump of muck at her feet. The silence lengthened. Obviously she was quite happy where she was.

"I'll do it." Seb made his way to the gate. "I'm ready for a change of scenery and some human conversation."

Caleb's face darkened, and he opened his mouth to speak, then seemed to think the better of it, and marched out of the shed. Seb nodded to Danny. "Thanks, Danny."

Seb could hardly keep up with Caleb as he made his way round to the parlour. His jaw was clenched tight. Seb had never seen Caleb angry, and there had been plenty of opportunities for him to lose his temper.

He didn't speak until the first cows were in the parlour and the clusters attached. "What does she see in that vet? How can she even make out a word he's saying?"

Seb shrugged. Diarmuid's County Kerry accent was very musical, but it wasn't easy at times to work out what he was asking.

"I can't believe she just chose to stay with *him* over helping *me*!"

"I think it's just a crush, Caleb. And I don't think he's at all interested in her. She's far too young for him. She just amuses him and makes a tedious job more bearable. That's all."

Caleb frowned. "That's not the point, Seb. I really thought she liked me. Now I'm not so sure."

Seb bit his lip. What was he supposed to say? "I think she still likes you."

"Huh!" Caleb grunted and turned round to work on the next row of cows. He was quiet for a long moment. "It's time for her to make up her mind."

Seb winced. He wasn't entirely sure what Caleb meant, but he didn't like the firm set of the young man's jaw.

Seb kicked off his boots at the back door and followed the others into the kitchen. He felt bone-weary, and his stomach growled at the delicious aroma of lasagne which filled the kitchen.

"Grab a seat, everyone," Aunt Karen called as she dished out generous portions onto each plate.

"Thanks, Mrs McRoss," Diarmuid said, throwing a crinkle-eyed smile in her direction. "This is much better than what I'd have been eating at home."

"Karen," she corrected warmly. " 'Mrs McRoss' makes me feel old."

"Diarmuid says he can only cook scrambled egg."

"Now, don't you give away all my secrets, Vinnie." Diarmuid winked at her as he spoke.

Seb glanced at Caleb. He'd chosen the seat farthest from the vet and was glowering at him, eyebrows lowered. Seb hoped Diarmuid would be able to make it through dinner without a plate of lasagne flying through the air towards him.

Uncle Matt gave God thanks for the food and they all tucked in. Diarmuid kept everyone amused with his stories of veterinary life.

"Honestly, Diarmuid," Aunt Karen exclaimed as she wiped tears of laughter from her eyes. "You should write a book. I think you're the Irish equivalent of James Herriot."

"Ah, I don't know about that." He leaned back in his seat and chuckled. "My grandfather was a vet in Kerry, back in the fifties and sixties. Now, his tales really were worth recording."

"Tell us some of them." Lavinia had pushed her plate to the side and was leaning forwards, eyes fixed on the vet. She seemed to have forgotten that Caleb was even in the room.

"Caleb." A soft voice spoke up across from Seb. "Are you cross?"

Caleb took a breath and glanced down at the little blonde girl beside him. He made an attempt at a smile. "Cross? No, Martha, I'm not cross."

She looked at him doubtfully. "You look a wee bit cross."

"I'm just trying to figure out what the vet is saying."

Danny snorted, but covered it with a cough when Caleb glared at him.

Martha nodded sagely. "Don't worry, Caleb. I haven't learned Irish yet. I don't understand him either."

Seb grinned at the exchange. He could understand why Martha would think that Diarmuid was speaking in the Irish language.

Caleb pushed his seat back. The legs screeched on the tiled floor. "Thanks, Karen. That was good, but I need to get back home." He turned to Matt. "I'll be here in the morning as usual for milking."

"Thanks, Caleb. I appreciate your help," Matt said. "Danny, yours too."

As the two young men left the kitchen, Seb glanced at Lavinia. She had barely registered their exit and was waiting for Diarmuid to finish his story. Seb hoped that things between Lavinia and Caleb would be back to normal soon. Maybe once this TB test was completed, she'd forget all about the handsome Kerry vet. Because, with Uncle Matt unable to work, they needed all the help they could get. They were already holding on by a slender thread. And if they couldn't work as a team, that thread would snap.

Chapter Nine

"So here's the two busy wee beavers home from school!" a familiar voice exclaimed as Seb and Lavinia stepped through the kitchen door. "I can't believe that the two o' you are runnin' a farm as well as goin' tae school an' doin' all your schoolwork."

Seb grinned. "Hello, Madge. It's good to see you again."

"An' you too, Seb. I was wile glad tae hear that ye moved away from the city. Full o' wickedness, thon big cities. Nowhere lik' this wee corner o' the world, ye know. Me an' Betty are just back from the south. She did the drivin', an' boy, was I thankful." She shook her head solemnly. "Thon traffic round Dublin was somethin' shockin'. I'd a been as lost as thon wee lass wi' the red coat in the forest if I was on my own."

Seb frowned. Who on earth was she talking about?

"Little Red Riding Hood?" asked Lavinia.

"The very one, Vinnie. I'd a been just lik' her. Lost an' about tae be ate by thon wolf that gobbled up the pigs."

"But, Madge, I don't think she was actually lost. And didn't the wolf wait until she was at her grandmother's house before he threatened to eat her?"

"Not in my day! They've changed these fairy stories that much. Took all the fun out o' them an' now ye'd hardly recognise them. Sure, that one about thon lassie wi' the nasty sisters–"

"How was your holiday?" Aunt Karen asked when Madge stopped to take a breath.

Madge flapped a large, rough hand in the air. "Karen, I'll tell ye no word o' a lie. Thon bed and breakfast was the strangest place I ever did set foot in." She leaned forwards and ominously lowered her voice. "In fact, I was near frightened out o' my wits before it was time tae go home." She shuddered. "Pictures o' creepy children in the bedroom an' hallways, an'," her eyes widened, "there was even a picture upside down."

Seb looked at Madge, bemused. "Why was it upside down? Did someone put it like that by mistake?"

"Huh!" Madge exclaimed. "No mistake at all. It was hung lik' that. *Deliberate!* I took it off the wall an' checked."

Lavinia turned to wash her hands, but not before Seb noticed her mouth threatening to break into a grin.

"An' what was worse, the place was filthy. An' the smell!" She wrinkled her nose. "I had tae give the room a good dust wi' my spare underslip an' it was fit for nothin' after that. Boysadear, I didn't know such places existed. An' it was 'highly recommended' in thon wee book too, I declare!" She shook her head disapprovingly. "The bed was that hard it was like sleepin' on the road. I don't think my back will ever recover."

"How was the food?" Seb asked.

"Ugh, Seb," she replied with an exasperated sigh. "Where would I ever start? The woman made a fry every mornin', but if ye left anythin', she heated it up for ye the next day!"

"How did she ever keep track of whose leftovers belonged to which person?"

Madge went wide-eyed. "Oh deary me, Vinnie! I never thought o' that! For all I know, I could a been eatin' a sausage that that whiskery oul body in the corner coughed an' haghed over. Oh, goodness knows how many infectious diseases are workin' away in my body as we speak!"

"How did Tommy get on with Sweep while you were away?" Uncle Matt asked from his seat at the head of the table. Seb was glad that the conversation had changed direction.

Madge folded her arms. "That man!" she exclaimed, infected sausages forgotten. "If he didn't go an' bring the dog into the house. An' after he'd been rollin' in cow dung!"

"Tommy? Rolling in cow dung?" Matt asked mischievously.

Madge frowned at Matt. "He might as well have been. The house was clean boggin' by the time I got back. Never again! It's not worth it. The good Lord didn't intend for us tae go chasin' here an' there anyway, I'm thinkin'." She leaned across and reached for another of

Aunt Karen's pineapple delights. "These are wile nice, Karen. I always had trouble gettin' them right. Ye'll have tae give me your recipe so I can see what I'm doin' wrong. An' Matt," she turned her attention to the head of the table, "how are you? Is the leg still sore? S'pose it would be, wouldn't it? When do they think ye'll be back tae normal? A while yet, probly. Did ye get the TB test done the other day?"

Matt opened his mouth to reply, but Madge was on a roll. "Tommy was wile sorry he couldn't help ye, but he's tae get a cataract off and he's waited that long tae hear about it. He struggles wile wi' readin', especially at night. An' driving! He can hardly see a thing anymore. When he meets a car, he has tae just stop. He says that the glare from their lights is somethin' shockin'. I told him tae ask the optician if new glasses would help, cause them ones he has are that badly scratched, but she said that it's the cataract. The glasses he has are just for readin' anyway and she said they'd be no good for seein'. I have bifocals. I don't really need them for seein' but I hate lookin' up from my crossword an' everythin' bein' blurry."

Seb glanced at Lavinia. She was finishing her pineapple delight with a look of puzzlement on her face. As entertaining as Madge's ramblings were, it was past milking time. He pushed his chair back and stood up.

"Ugh, are ye away, son?" Madge asked. "Well, all the best. How are ye getting' on at the new school? Everybody treating ye okay? It's no' a bad school, that. I mine–"

"Seb, Vinnie, if you're finished, head on upstairs and get changed." Matt rescued the young people.

"Oh, am I keepin' ye back? I'm wile sorry. I better head on an' get back tae get the dinner on. See what thon pup is at. He's a rascal, that one. I gave him a cushion off that oul sofa in the shed, an' here if he didn't chew it tae bits. I was findin' stuffin' for weeks! But," she waved a hand at Seb and Lavinia, "I better let ye go. Mind an' come across an' see us sometime. When ye have a minute. We miss havin' ye drop in, ye know."

"If she isn't away when we go back down, should we escape out the front door?" Lavinia giggled as they dashed up the stairs to change.

"Maybe we should bring her with us to the milking parlour. The cows could do with a little light entertainment these days."

"Infectious sausages!" he heard Lavinia chuckle as she entered her bedroom, and he couldn't help but smile. There was nothing like a good dose of Madge to lift one's spirits.

Seb breathed in the wholesome aroma of cows as he stood wiping down udders. Comforting and welcoming. He certainly wouldn't have used those words this time last year, but a lot could change in a few short months. He had to laugh now when he remembered how frightened he'd been and how he'd assumed that Mirabelle, the big friendly giant of a cow, was out to kill him. Now he was actually becoming attached to the large animals. He frowned as he caught sight of the trimmed injection sites on the neck of the cow who'd just entered the parlour. They were so busy that they hardly had time to think these days, but the second part of the TB test loomed over them like a thick, black cloud, filled with torrential rain, thunder and lightning. Once more, Seb prayed that the cloud would pass over and not unleash its storm on Cherryhill Farm. The thought of having reactors to the test was more than Seb wanted to imagine.

He shoved the thought away. Worrying about it wasn't going to change the outcome.

"Diarmuid says Freddy Robertson Jr's moustache looks like something somebody who's advertising car insurance would have," Lavinia said.

Seb groaned. Diarmuid again. The vet was a very pleasant chap, but Seb didn't want Vinnie getting carried away. "I don't think Caleb is too keen on Diarmuid."

"What?" Lavinia swung around, knocking her head on the glass jar full of milk. She rubbed her temple and winced. "Why doesn't he like him?"

Seb shrugged. "Maybe something to do with the way you ignored him yesterday?"

She looked down and frowned. "Did I?" She bit her lip.

Seb removed the clusters and sprayed the teats with disinfectant spray. He figured that Lavinia could work out the answer to that question by herself.

Aunt Karen had packed both Martha and Uncle Matt off to bed, and headed out to a natural skincare products evening. Seb yawned and leaned his elbow on the kitchen table. He wished he could head to bed as well instead of trying to catch up on his maths homework. The teachers had been very understanding, but Seb knew their patience would only last so long. If he didn't catch up soon, he would never pass the exams in the new year.

Lavinia's phone lit up and she lifted it, then swiped and tapped at the screen. After setting it down, she lifted her pen again and began to chew the end. She flicked through the textbook, pushed it away, lifted her notebook, set it down and rummaged in her school bag.

Seb looked at her. What on earth was up with her?

The sound of a car pulling into the yard caused her to throw her pen down and head for the door.

"Where are you going?" asked Seb.

"Out to check a cow. I think she's going to calve tonight."

"Wait! Who's that?"

"It's Caleb," she turned and hissed. "Don't go yelling it all over the country. I need to talk to him." She looked a little sheepish.

Seb shook his head and went back to his homework.

An hour later, his maths homework and a short geography assignment completed, Seb yawned and stretched. Lavinia still hadn't returned, so he thought he'd better go and check on the cow himself.

Seb pulled on his coat and wellies and made his way to the calving pen. As he reached the shed, he heard voices.

"But, Caleb, you know what Dad will say! He keeps saying I'm too young and he doesn't want me to make a mistake and get my heart broken." Lavinia sounded distraught.

"So don't tell him!" Caleb's voice was sharp.

"That won't work. You know that. You're here so much; they'll figure it out."

"Well, I'm fed up waiting. When *will* you be old enough? They certainly think you're old enough to hang about with a County Kerry vet for hours on end."

"Caleb, we've been over this already. I told you, I don't like Diarmuid that way. He's just... a nice person."

"Well, nice person or not, if you really wanted to be my girlfriend, you would."

"I'll ask Dad in the morning. I promise." Lavinia sounded on the verge of tears. Seb winced. Shouldn't this have been a romantic moment? He heard footsteps and turned to go back to the house. He was getting far too good at hearing things he wasn't supposed to hear.

"Seb?" Lavinia's voice echoed in the shed.

"I was just wondering how the cow was doing." He turned back and walked closer. "I guess it's all under control."

Lavinia peered at him suspiciously, then relaxed a little when Seb gave no indication of overhearing their conversation. "She's okay for a couple of hours. I'll check her then, if you check a couple of hours after that."

Seb nodded. "All right, then. Good night, Vinnie. See you in the morning, Caleb."

Seb walked back to the yard. He wasn't looking forward to the confrontation between Matt and Lavinia in the morning. No one needed this, especially not now.

Chapter Ten

Morning milking was a silent, somewhat frosty affair. It was Seb's morning to help Caleb in the parlour, but the older boy only gave monosyllabic answers to Seb's attempts to make conversation. There was so much that was wrong with this situation. Caleb seemed driven by jealousy to claim Lavinia, while she was only agreeing to ask her dad's permission to prove to Caleb that she had no feelings for Diarmuid. Caleb and Lavinia had always seemed like a natural match, but this didn't feel right to Seb. *Although what would I know about it*, he thought wryly. His only experience had been what he'd observed at school in Belfast, which wasn't exactly the gold standard for romantic relationships, to put it mildly.

The last cow left the parlour. "I can manage on my own from here," Caleb said. "You'll need to get ready for school."

"Thanks, Caleb." Seb stripped off his gloves and dumped them in the bin, then washed his hands and arms before making his way to the house. There was no sign of Lavinia.

As he entered the house, he could hear voices from behind the closed office door. Uncle Matt, and – he strained to hear as he prised off his wellies – Lavinia. Seb winced. He'd better get upstairs before he managed to hear anything he shouldn't – again!

When he came back downstairs after showering and changing into his uniform, Uncle Matt was sitting at the table, his leg resting on one of the other chairs, and Aunt Karen was stirring something in a saucepan on the stove. Martha had a page and a few colouring pencils and was drawing what appeared to be a cow, if the black splodges on the circle in the middle of the page were any indication.

"Everything go okay, Seb?" Uncle Matt looked up from his paper. If Lavinia had talked to him about what Seb assumed she had, Uncle Matt didn't seem at all bothered. Maybe he'd decided it was no big deal and had given in after all.

"Yes. Caleb is finishing off."

"Vinnie was saying the cow calved during the night."

Seb nodded and stifled a yawn. "She was ready to calve when I got up to check on her. It was pretty straightforward."

"That's good." Uncle Matt sat back in his seat and put his paper down. "Still three due this week?" He looked worried.

"Yes. I didn't get asking Vinnie yet how the others are looking. Hope they don't all go at once."

Uncle Matt gave a wry chuckle. "Let's hope not."

Aunt Karen began to spoon scrambled eggs onto each plate.

"Did you arrange with Tommy which days he's coming?"

Uncle Matt folded the paper and threw it onto the kitchen bench where it landed on top of the opened egg carton. "Whoops!"

"Matt!" Aunt Karen scolded.

Uncle Matt grinned up at her. "Sorry, darling!"

She shook her head in exasperation and sighed, but patted him affectionately on the shoulder as she set his plate of eggs in front of him.

"By the looks of it, Vinnie seems to be very behind with her homework, so Tommy has agreed to come this evening for milking so she can get caught up a bit. Then, from next week, as well as coming round on some weekday mornings to help with the feeding and bedding, he's going to help with evening milking on Mondays and Thursdays, so that will at least give you each an afternoon off per week. Just until I'm back on my feet. I'm pretty sure I could get back to milking again when I don't have to keep the leg up all the time."

"You what? Matt McRoss! Get that idea out of your head this minute!" Aunt Karen's eyes were flashing. "Do you want to further injure yourself and do permanent damage?" She blew out a huff of breath. "Farmers have got to be the most foolhardy people on this earth."

Footsteps sounded on the stairs and seconds later Lavinia appeared in the kitchen. Seb looked up as she entered. If Uncle Matt looked as though his morning had been completely calm and normal, Lavinia certainly didn't look the same way. Her eyes were swollen and puffy, and she would only look at her toes.

Aunt Karen's eyes opened wide in alarm and she opened her mouth to speak, but Seb noticed Uncle Matt's hand subtly grab her arm, accompanied with a small shake of his head.

Lavinia's request had obviously not been approved after all.

"There you are, Lavinia. We're just ready to eat," Aunt Karen said softly.

"Not hungry." Lavinia's voice was thick.

"Try some anyway." Aunt Karen slid the plate in front of her daughter.

Uncle Matt gave thanks for the food and, apart from Lavinia, they all tucked in. She pushed the egg around the plate with her fork. Her hair hung down to hide her face.

"Vinnie, are you okay?" Martha asked, staring at her big sister.

"I'm fine."

Martha's eyes were big and solemn. "It's wrong to tell lies."

"Who says it's wrong to tell lies? Who makes up these rules anyway?" snapped Lavinia.

Seb heard Aunt Karen take a sharp breath. What had got into Lavinia? He knew things were stressful these days, and obviously things hadn't gone well this morning, but he'd never heard her say such things before.

"Lavinia!" Uncle Matt's voice was firm and filled with warning.

Lavinia shoved her plate away. "Sorry," she mumbled.

Uncle Matt reached for his Bible. "Let's have our Bible reading before you two go to catch the bus." He flicked through the pages and began to read. " 'My son, do not forget my law, but let your heart keep my commands; for length of days and long life and peace will they add to you. Let not mercy and truth forsake you; bind them around your neck, write them on the tablet of your heart, and so find favour and high esteem in the sight of God and man. Trust in the Lord with all your heart, and lean not on your own understanding; in all your ways acknowledge Him, and He shall direct your paths...' "

Trust in the Lord with all your heart...

Seb let the words seep into his brain. Everything felt so out of control these days. They were so busy that there was hardly time to think, and when he did, his thoughts were full of worries and fears. It was a timely reminder, to rest on the Lord, to cast all his worries on Him, and instead of trying to work things out by himself, to let himself be guided by the Lord.

"Vinnie..." Seb began as they waited for the bus.

"Don't talk to me." Her eyes were a little less puffy, but she still looked miserable. The others on the bus were sure to notice. She gave a half-hearted wave at Tommy as he arrived in his old Defender and turned into the lane. Seb was glad that the old neighbour was able to help – it certainly took a lot of the pressure off them on school mornings.

The bus appeared in the distance and finally pulled up beside them. Lavinia reluctantly walked down the bus to her usual seat while Seb paid the driver. Carl's squeaky voice travelled to the front of the bus. "What's wrong with you, Vinnie?"

As he made his way down the bus, Seb watched her shrug, then slouch down in her seat and turn towards the window.

When Rebekah got on, Lavinia continued to stare out the window and hardly acknowledged her friend. "Vinnie, is everything all right?" she asked in concern.

"Allergies," she sniffed.

"Allergies?" Rebekah glanced across the aisle at Seb.

He shook his head and shrugged.

When the bus reached the school gates, Lavinia was the last off the bus. Seb and Rebekah waited for her, but she walked past them and marched into school on her own.

"Seb, what is wrong with Vinnie today? I've never seen her like this."

How much should he say? Rebekah's brother was the main cause of Lavinia's foul mood. And, after all, he really shouldn't know anything about it anyway.

"I think the stress of the farm is getting to her a bit. We haven't time for anything these days, and the vet's coming back to read the TB test results tomorrow."

"But did something trigger some sort of a meltdown? This is a bit dramatic for Vinnie!"

Seb let a few seconds pass before he answered. "Yes. Something else has happened. But I shouldn't even know about it." The automatic doors slid open and they walked through.

"That's okay, Seb. You don't need to tell me. I pray for Vinnie's salvation anyway, but I'll make this a special matter for prayer too." Her blue eyes were full of compassion.

"Thanks." Lavinia didn't know how blessed she was, having a friend like Rebekah, someone who didn't only care for her as a friend, but had a deep concern for her soul.

As they made their way to the form room for roll call, he looked around to see where Lavinia had gone. She seemed to have disappeared. They entered the room and took their seats. Danny was at a desk at the back, watching something on his phone. Seb went over to join him and Danny looked up.

"Have you seen this, Seb? This is a clip of a DVD that's coming out near Christmas. It's about one of the largest silaging contractors in the whole of Ireland."

Seb leaned over and watched the footage. He wasn't keen on the music the producers had used, but it looked like something he'd like to watch. Maybe when it came out, things would be back to normal and there would be time to do something as relaxing as watching a silaging DVD.

The door to the classroom opened and Lavinia came in, followed by Jasmine. Seb frowned. Jasmine seemed pleasant, but her attitude and her obsession with her appearance reminded Seb of many of the girls at his last school. Lavinia certainly looked a bit happier, but Seb didn't like the uncomfortable feeling in the pit of his stomach. Why would Lavinia ignore Rebekah and spend time with Jasmine? Seb had assumed that Lavinia would have been pouring out her complaints about the situation to her best friend, especially since it was her friend's brother with whom she'd been obsessed for so long.

Mr Marsden entered the room and made his way to the desk. As he began roll call, Seb pushed the thoughts away. He'd try to figure it out some other time.

Chapter Eleven

"What on earth is going on?!" Aunt Karen stood up from the table and peered out of the window. Jess's loud barks were interspersed with fierce yips from Glen.

"See anything?" Uncle Matt asked.

"Someone's here. But I don't recognise the car." She made her way to the door. "Jess! Glen! Stop that barking this instant."

The barks died down for a few seconds, then recommenced with more ferocity. Seb could hear Jess growling. It wasn't unusual for the dogs to bark at strange cars, but Seb had never actually heard them growl at anyone before.

"Jess! Lie down!" Aunt Karen commanded, and finally the noise subsided. In the silence, Seb could hear a man's voice, then an exclamation of surprise from Karen.

Seconds later, she stepped back into the kitchen, followed by a tall, dark-haired man.

As she stepped aside, Seb gasped. He knew Uncle Matt didn't have any brothers, but the man in the doorway could have been Uncle Matt's identical twin.

"Dale!" Matt exclaimed, as he dropped his leg to the floor and fumbled for his crutches. "What are you doing here? Last I heard you were in New Zealand." He gave a laugh and struggled to his feet, then clapped the man on the back as he gave him a bear hug. Despite the strong similarity, the stranger wasn't quite as tall as Matt, and of a less muscular build.

The man laughed. "Never know who the wind blows in, Matt." His smile disappeared and he frowned. "But what has happened to you?"

Matt gave a dismissive wave. "Little accident with an angry bull." He lowered himself to his chair again. "Have a seat. We're just in the middle of tea and cake. Sorry about those dogs."

Dale smiled sheepishly as he pulled out a chair. "I bring out the worst in dogs for some reason. Always did."

Matt laughed. "True! I'd forgotten that." He glanced around the table at the stunned faces. "Everybody, this is my cousin, Dale Maxwell."

"Pleased to meet you." Lavinia smiled across the table at the man.

"You must be Lavinia. I remember hearing that your parents had named you after your grandmother – my Aunt Lavinia. Matt's mother and my mother were sisters."

Lavinia nodded. "You can call me Vinnie if you like. Most people do."

Dale turned to Seb. "And you are…?"

"I'm Seb. My mum is Aunt Karen's sister."

"So Vinnie doesn't have a twin that I never heard of," Dale chuckled.

"Oh, gracious, no!" laughed Aunt Karen. "Lavinia provides us with enough teenage drama all by herself."

Seb glanced at his cousin. She had looked down and was toying with the handle of her mug, but he saw a flicker of something pass across her face. Aunt Karen had inadvertently touched a tender spot with her words.

"How long are you here for?" Matt asked Dale as he reached for the plate of sponge cake Aunt Karen was handing to him. "Or are you back for good?"

Dale chuckled. "No, just a visit. I plan to go back at the end of the year, but we'll see how things go."

"You must have a great boss that gives you so much time off and is flexible too," remarked Lavinia.

Dale smiled at her. "I do. He said that my job will be there for me when I get back."

"What do you do?" Seb broke off a piece of the cake with his fork and popped it into his mouth.

"I help manage a large dairy herd on the South Island."

"A dairy herd!" exclaimed Lavinia.

"Dale and I were both daft about cows growing up," said Uncle Matt. "We spent most of our summer holidays here at Cherryhill."

"So what do you plan to do when you're here?" Lavinia leaned forwards towards Dale.

"I want to take a trip to Donegal to see my sister, and my visit is coinciding with a school reunion, but I haven't planned more than that just yet."

"And where are you staying?"

"Lavinia," Aunt Karen broke in. "Try not to bombard Dale with questions. You're being a little intense."

Lavinia sat back in her chair. "Sorry, Dale. It's just… " She broke off as she caught her mother's eye.

"If you're finished, I think you should go and catch up on some of that schoolwork you said you were so behind with, and Seb, Tommy will be here any minute, so maybe you should make a start on the milking."

"It's a pity I don't have any working clothes with me, or I'd be tempted to come out and help too. Have you made many changes to the farm?" Dale turned to Matt.

Seb pushed his chair back from the table and made his way upstairs to change. He knew exactly what Lavinia was thinking. Dale worked on a dairy unit, and he didn't have to go back until the end of the year – maybe by then Uncle Matt would be back on his feet. He wondered if Uncle Matt would ask Dale to stay. Having someone else to run the farm would be such a weight off their shoulders, and would let Seb get caught up at school. Maybe he could even go back to live with his mum in the house he'd barely slept a night in since arriving from Belfast.

"Tommy," Seb called above the noise of the milking machines. He waited until the old man's grey head turned in his direction. "Two of the cows look ready to calve."

Two?" Tommy chuckled. "Poor Vinnie. She'll not get much homework done tonight!"

"I'm going to get her. Will you be okay in the meantime?"

Tommy nodded and waved, then continued wiping down udders.

Seb left the parlour and raced across the yard. He hoped that Dale would still be there and would be willing to help out, but the blue Hyundai was gone.

Uncle Matt looked up as he entered the kitchen. "Something wrong, Seb?"

"Two cows are about to calve. I need to get Vinnie."

Uncle Matt swung his leg off the chair. "Hand me my crutches, Seb."

"Matt, you aren't going out there," Aunt Karen told him.

"I can at least supervise."

Aunt Karen had already begun shaking her head. "No way. I know what you're like. You'll end up on the ground with a cow on top of you and that leg will never work again." She turned to Seb. "I'll get Vinnie."

As she left the room, Matt spoke again. "If things aren't going smoothly, come and tell me at once. At least I can come and assess if we need the vet or not."

Seb looked at his uncle. Frustration showed on every line in his face. Seb figured it must be soul-destroying for a hardworking man like Uncle Matt to have to pass the time in the house while a couple of teenagers kept the farm running.

“This won’t be forever, Uncle Matt.”

“I hope not, Seb. I’m going stir-crazy as it is, and I’m not even home from hospital a week, not to mention the way that this has disrupted your life.”

“It wasn’t your fault.” He looked down at his wellies that he’d forgotten to take off when he burst into the house. “It was mine.”

Seb glanced up to catch Uncle Matt frowning at him. “Seb, there’s no way this was your fault. I should have known never to trust a bull, and if he’d got you instead of me, you could easily have been killed. Stop blaming yourself. You do far more for this farm than you have any need to do. I really appreciate it, you know.”

Seb glanced at his uncle. From the minute he’d met Uncle Matt, when Seb was full of rebellion and hurt, he’d known that he was sincere and genuine, calm and unwavering in his confidence in God. The recent happenings had buffeted him, and Seb had realised that his uncle was still human, but the secret of his strength remained the same. Seb knew that Uncle Matt found the current situation exceptionally trying, yet he still rested on God.

A clatter down the stairs interrupted Seb’s thoughts. “So they’re both calving at the same time?” Lavinia asked. “I might have known. Only one was due today, but those two are twins and you never see one without the other." She dashed into the office for her coat and wellies.

"I'd better get back to helping Tommy with the milking. Shout if you need either of us." Seb headed out the door and back to the parlour. They might just be able to manage if the cows weren't calving, or the TB test hadn't been this week, but those two things made the farm go from busy to almost unmanageable.

He slid open the door to the parlour. He was exhausted, but he had to keep going. At the minute, there really wasn't any other option. As he worked, he prayed. For the calving cows, for Vinnie and for Uncle Matt.

"Two heifers, Dad." Lavinia flopped into her seat at the table and wiped her arm across her face.

Seb watched Uncle Matt smile. "All go okay?"

"More or less. I couldn't keep an eye on both, so Tommy left Seb to the milking and calved one of them."

It had been a busy evening's milking, trying to keep up on his own, but it was clear that Tommy had much more experience calving cows than he had.

"What we really need," Lavinia looked up at her dad innocently, "is someone who can live here for the next couple of months. Someone with a bit of experience in dairying."

"And where on earth would we find such a person?" he replied, just as innocently.

"Uh, Dad!" Lavinia rolled her eyes. "Did you even *ask* Dale if he could help?"

"Lavinia, Dale is here on a holiday. What makes you think he wants to work?"

Aunt Karen lifted two plates from the bottom oven of the Aga and carried them to the table. "I kept your dinner warm. I hope it's still okay."

Seb's stomach rumbled. It could be as dried out as an old boot and he really wouldn't care right now. He bowed his head and silently gave thanks for his meal, then dug into the lamb chops and rice.

Uncle Matt glanced at Aunt Karen, then began to speak. "Vinnie, you know that phrase about counting chickens before they hatch, but I made Dale aware of our predicament. He didn't know about my accident, and I never knew he was even planning to visit from New Zealand. We were best buddies growing up, but we lost touch when I headed to university and he went travelling. He ended up in New Zealand and has only been back a handful of times."

"So what did he say?" Lavinia asked impatiently.

"He said he'd think about it. He's going to visit his sister, Clarissa, this weekend, so he's to let me know on Monday."

"If he hardly ever sees her, won't he want to stay there longer than a weekend?"

Uncle Matt laughed. "I wouldn't think so, somehow. Dale and Clarissa never really got on, and I can't imagine much will have changed. She's a creative person. Pottery or weaving or something like that. The last time I spoke to her she told me that she liked the solitude of the wilds of Donegal. Dale will shatter that solitude, and I don't think she'll appreciate it."

"The only thing is, Seb, that if Dale comes here, we'll have to give him your room." Aunt Karen looked sympathetically at him.

Seb shrugged. "That's okay, Aunt Karen. It'll be good to go back to live with Mum."

"I thought you'd like to do that if you aren't needed to work so much, but if it turns out that you do need to stay here, we can move the girls into one room."

Seb glanced at Lavinia and almost laughed at the comical look of horror on her face.

"Anyway, we'll see what Dale says on Monday."

"Monday. By then, the TB test will be over." Lavinia grimaced. "I'm dreading it, to be perfectly honest. Some of those girls look like reactors for sure."

Uncle Matt rubbed a hand through his hair. "I'm not looking forward to it either, Vinnie. I don't remember ever having known of so much TB around the country and we've never had adjoining neighbours with it. I think we need to prepare ourselves."

Seb swallowed hard. The harsh reality of what could go wrong was sinking in. He would pray. Hard. This family had gone through enough already. Surely God would hear and preserve them. He had to.

Chapter Twelve

Tense. That was the only word Seb could come up with to describe the atmosphere today. Gone was Lavinia's light-hearted chatter to Diarmuid. Tommy was wordlessly getting on with the task of herding cattle into the yard. Diarmuid was professional and calm, yet even he seemed to be dreading the outcome.

Diarmuid had brought a student vet this time to record the results – a pale sort, who didn't look as if there were too many brains behind his sleepy eyes. There had to be brains in his head, though, Seb thought, or he'd never have got into veterinary school. As long as he could take down the measurements Diarmuid called out, that was all that he needed to do today.

As Diarmuid gathered his equipment and got ready to begin, Seb took a breath and silently prayed. Uncle Matt had prayed earlier that all would go according to God's perfect will. Seb was finding that prayer difficult. He'd rather pray that not one of the cows would have TB. God could still work miracles, after all. Had everyone forgotten that?

The cows began to make their way through the long, narrow chute.

The first cow entered the crush and Diarmuid measured the skin at both injection sites. He called the numbers to the student, who frowned at the page, then recorded them. "She's fine."

Seb breathed a prayer of relief. One down, a few hundred to go.

The cow was released and the next cow entered the crush. The process was repeated. Eleven cows had passed through the crush and been cleared, when Seb noticed Diarmuid and the student confer. Diarmuid shook his head.

Seb's heart dropped to his boots like a lead weight in a pond. They had a reactor.

Uncle Matt made his way out to the shed as the second reactor was being steered towards a holding pen. He looked sad but not surprised. "How many so far, Seb?" he asked, as Seb walked over to the gate to speak to him.

"This is only the second. He also said something about an inconclusive."

Uncle Matt nodded. "That's where they can't tell for sure if she has TB or not. What they do with her will depend on how many reactors we have."

"Maybe that will be all there is."

"No. There'll be more." Uncle Matt pointed to a white cow with a few scattered black spots. "Look at her neck."

Seb studied the cow. He wasn't sure how he hadn't noticed the huge bulge at the lower injection site.

"She's not the most attractive cow, but she has one of the highest yields in the herd. I'll be sorry to see her go."

Seb shuddered. He hadn't thought past today. It was just dawning on him that Diarmuid's measurements spelled a death sentence for any of these ladies who happened to react to the bovine tuberculin injection.

"Do you want to go beside Diarmuid?" asked Seb. "We could get you a couple of chairs and you could put your leg up."

"Better do that, or your aunt will be down on me like a ton of bricks again. I never realised that Karen was such a worrier until this happened." He smiled wryly.

"She's just concerned about you."

"I know that, Seb. Between you and me, I wish she would lay off the worrying for a wee while. It's getting a bit suffocating."

Once he'd his uncle placed near the crush, he returned to helping Tommy move the cows forwards.

Uncle Matt was right. The white cow was a reactor, as was another of his high-yielding cows. He didn't want to think about the cows being culled, nor about the huge loss of income for the farm.

Caleb arrived to help with the milking and Tommy joined him. Seb's jaw felt sore and he realised he was gritting his teeth. He felt as if he were watching a disaster unfolding in a movie, yet was unable to look away.

The milking cows done, Diarmuid began to work on the heifers. Seb glanced at Lavinia. She was pale and she had a worried frown on her face. They already had far too many reactors.

Seb herded the next heifer into the crush. Lavinia's heifer. Her pride and joy. Runner up this year at the agricultural show, and predicted to be the winner next year. Diarmuid measured the two sites and shook his head. "I'm sorry, Vinnie."

Lavinia's face crumpled and she turned away, shoulders shaking.

Seb felt sick and he clutched the nearest railing. *Why, God? Why?*

The student vet opened the crush and guided the heifer to the holding pen with the rest. Seb heard a great, gasping sob over the noise of the remaining cattle. Uncle Matt grabbed his crutches and staggered to his feet. He made his way to his daughter and turned her around, then held her as she wept.

In the end, there were eighteen reactors, including Lavinia's heifer. Eighteen valuable animals, all destined for slaughter. Seb leaned his arms on the gate and watched them, their large dark eyes curious and trusting. They had no idea that their days were numbered, that the thickness of skin on their necks had determined their future.

He heard footsteps behind him and turned to see Lavinia. "Vinnie..." Seb didn't know what to say.

A wobbly sigh broke from her and her eyes filled with tears. "It's so unfair," she murmured. "That heifer is one of the best we've ever had, and she hasn't even had her calf yet. Never mind the fact I've got so attached to her, we're going to lose that bloodline that we worked so hard to build."

Seb frowned. He hadn't even considered the loss of bloodlines. Some of these cows would have sisters, or daughters, or nieces, but others were valuable because of their unique, well-planned genetics. He was relieved that Mirabelle, his favourite cow, was clear, but felt deeply sorry that Lavinia had had such a devastating blow.

"I just don't understand why this had to happen," she went on. "Haven't we gone through enough already? Dad's accident and now this on the top of it all."

Seb was silent. He'd had the same thoughts. Why would God let this happen? Why didn't He work a miracle and protect Cherryhill Farm from TB? Seb had no doubt that this would have been possible. He knew that God is a God who works wonders.

"I don't know, Vinnie. I have to be honest and say that I don't know why God would let this happen."

Lavinia sniffed. "I'm starting to think that He doesn't care about us at all."

"Vinnie! You know that isn't true." Seb was alarmed.

She shrugged and continued watching the cows. "Did you know that this result means we can't move cattle off this farm until we get two clear tests, one in sixty days and the second sixty days after that?"

Seb frowned and did the maths. "So, providing we get the two clear tests, we can't move cattle until March?"

Lavinia sighed again. "Yes, and we've cows calving. Those new bull calves? We can't sell them until then. It's not financially viable to keep them when they need so much feed, but we don't have any other option right now."

"And if we don't get a clear test?"

"Then the movement restriction lasts until we manage to get two clear tests."

"But, Vinnie, this could go on for years!"

Lavinia nodded. "Exactly. It's a nightmare. And how many more cows might we lose before then?"

"That's crazy!" Seb hadn't even considered the long-term effects of a positive TB result.

She snorted. "Try telling that to the be-nice-to-animals brigade who insist that we shouldn't cull badgers because they have nothing to do with the spread of TB. They don't seem to care that while the badgers carry TB from farm to farm, hundreds of thousands of cattle have been slaughtered. Aren't cattle animals too? And," Lavinia was on a roll, "what about those farms which have been in the family for years, and then are wiped out by TB? It's devastating."

Seb considered Lavinia's words. It was sickeningly unfair. Why wasn't something more being done?

"We should likely go in for dinner. Mum will be wondering where we are."

"Are the others staying for dinner?"

"No. Everyone has gone. They had plans for this evening, apart from Caleb, and well... "

Seb glanced at Lavinia. He could guess why Caleb didn't want to stay.

"Did you hear anything the other night when you came out to check on the cow?" She didn't look at Seb as she spoke, instead concentrating on opening the gate.

Seb paused. He hated admitting to eavesdropping, but he needed to tell the truth. "I heard the end of your conversation. I'm sorry. I didn't mean to."

Lavinia gave a dry laugh. "I thought you did. So you can guess that Dad said no, then."

"I thought as much." He hesitated, unsure if he should continue. "How did Caleb react?"

"I didn't get talking to him before we went off to school, so I texted him later. He was so angry."

"Is he still angry?"

Lavinia shrugged. "I haven't seen him much." They'd reached the yard and she paused before climbing the steps. "That night he got so mad – I'd never seen him like that before. It made me kind of scared."

Seb frowned. Why had Caleb acted like that? Surely if he liked Lavinia enough to want her to be his girlfriend, why would he frighten her? He'd always looked up to Caleb, considered him a friend. He'd liked his calm, easy-going manner. He hadn't even got cross when Seb had persuaded them to find the cattle rustlers and it all turned out so badly. But now that he'd scared Lavinia and had added to her problems, Seb wasn't at all sure that he really liked Caleb that much anymore.

"I think your dad was right to say no," he said, as Lavinia put her hand on the handle to enter the house.

She turned back and looked at him. Her expression was almost unreadable, but Seb caught a faint glimpse of something in her eyes as she gave a slight nod.

Something that looked very much like relief.

Chapter Thirteen

"Dad, did you know who's back doing the milk collection?" Lavinia called through the office door as she prised off her wellies in the back porch.

Uncle Matt looked up from the open spreadsheet on the computer. "I heard Trevor was driving again. I didn't think they would give him back his old job."

Lavinia padded into the office and slid onto the floor, her back against the metal filing cabinet. "He's big mates with the manager and I think he pulled a few strings."

Seb leaned against the doorframe, intrigued by the conversation. "What happened?"

"Dad reported him for drunk driving." Lavinia's tone was matter-of-fact.

Seb's eyes opened wide. "When? And what did he say about that?"

Uncle Matt twisted around to look at Seb. "A few years ago. He came tearing up the lane and almost knocked down a wall at the side of the yard. The minute he opened the door of the cab there was no doubt what the cause of the erratic driving was."

"But that wasn't the first time you'd smelled drink off him, Dad."

"No, it wasn't. I'd phoned the company before and all they'd say was that they'd look into it. That day, I phoned the police, and they breathalysed him down the road. He was well over the limit. It's a miracle he didn't kill someone."

"Did he ever find out who reported him?"

"I don't know. I think he figured it out. I saw him in the supermarket about a month after it happened."

"Dad, tell Seb what he did." Lavinia had leaned forwards in expectation.

Uncle Matt chuckled. "He was with his girlfriend, a wee slight brunette with skyscraper heels. The minute he saw me I noticed his fists clench and the veins start to pop out on his arms–"

"He's all into bodybuilding," interjected Lavinia. "He's got a shaved head and a neck like a Charolais bull."

"I didn't think Charolais bulls had shaved heads," Seb said, trying to keep his face straight.

"Of course they don't! It's his neck that's like a bull, not his head. Anyway, Dad was trying to tell you what happened."

Seb refrained from pointing out that it had actually been Lavinia who had interrupted.

Uncle Matt smiled. "As I was saying, he started getting all mad, red-faced and shaking, then the girlfriend grabbed hold of his arm. I don't know what she thought she was going to do, because he started to stride towards me with her hanging from his arm, and the tips of her pointy-toed shoes trailing along the ground. I didn't want a scene in the supermarket, so I dumped my groceries onto the nearest shelf and headed out the door. I think the security guard got him stopped."

"Better keep him out of your way when he's here then."

Lavinia crossed her legs and began to pick sawdust from her socks. "I think he's forgotten it. Tommy said he was talking to him the other morning and he was all smiles. Asked how you were, Dad."

"Maybe he was thinking 'it serves him right'."

She snorted. "Who knows? Tommy said he seemed concerned."

"Well, maybe now he's got his job back he's forgiven me." Uncle Matt raised his eyebrows. He didn't look too convinced.

"How many are due to calve next week?" Seb gestured to the spreadsheet.

"Two. Maybe everyone will get a bit of a reprieve. This is turning out to be another busy week for you all."

"I thought Dale was supposed to be back today." Lavinia swept the pieces of sawdust into a little pile.

"He decided to stay in Donegal for a few more days, but he'll be here before the weekend. He says he's happy to come and help."

Seb smiled. "That's great, Uncle Matt."

"He'll have to take over your room, Seb."

"That's no problem. I'll get it cleared out…"

Lavinia laughed. "I think Dale had better wait a while."

Seb frowned at his cousin. The room was messy, granted. But

what did she expect when he hardly had time to breathe between farm work and school. And, speaking of school, he really ought to go and finish that English assignment. He'd started it while Tommy and Lavinia did the milking, but had taken a break to go and feed the calves. He'd stayed out there far too long, watching the long-legged little animals greedily slurp their buckets of milk.

Lavinia pushed herself up from the floor and stretched. "I need to get some maths done for tomorrow or Mrs Craig will go ballistic."

Her dad pointed at the neat pile of sawdust. "You can take your rubbish with you."

Lavinia gave a sheepish grin, then bent down to lift the pieces and dump them in the wastepaper basket beside the desk. She brushed past Seb and headed for the kitchen. Seb turned to follow, but stopped when he heard Uncle Matt's voice.

"Seb, grab a seat. I've hardly had a chance to talk to you since you got back."

Seb went through to the kitchen and lifted a chair from under the kitchen table. After carrying it through to the study, he propped it against the wall and plopped himself onto it.

"So how are things going at school?" Uncle Matt began.

"Fine. I like it better than my last school. Most of the teachers are really nice, and it's great having other Christians in my class."

Uncle Matt smiled. "That is a big bonus." He paused. "I'm sure your mum will be glad to have you back."

Seb nodded. He tried to phone her every day during lunch at school. He felt sorry that she'd mostly been on her own since moving away from Belfast, but she'd been very good about letting him stay at Cherryhill to help.

"So what have you been looking at lately in your Bible study?"

Seb scratched his head as he tried to recall. He'd read through quite a few chapters this week, but he hadn't had any opportunity to look at anything in depth since... "Baptism."

Uncle Matt chuckled. "Well, now, Seb. That's a good study. Had you any questions?"

"Loads. I was reading Acts chapter eight. Philip was explaining a passage in Isaiah to the man from Ethiopia, and all of a sudden the man asks for baptism. I assume he got saved before he asked?"

"That's right, Seb. What does Philip say to him? 'If you believe with all your heart, you may.' And the Ethiopian man replies in the affirmative. Baptism is for believers. It's always associated with salvation in the Bible, although not necessary for salvation. Maybe you can think of at least one person in the Bible who was saved but not baptised."

Seb frowned.

"I'll give you a clue. He died very soon after he was saved."

"Oh! The thief on the cross beside the Lord Jesus."

"That's him. He went to heaven even though he was never baptised, but it's God's will that all believers should be baptised. Do you know what it means to be baptised?"

"Is it going underneath the water?" Seb asked.

"That's true. The word 'baptise' comes from a Greek word which means to dip or immerse. It's a picture of the death, burial and resurrection of the Lord Jesus. When believers are baptised, it is a symbol that, when we were saved, we died with Christ, were buried with Him and were raised to walk in newness of life, as it says in Romans 6. It's an outward sign of an inward change."

Seb considered what Uncle Matt had just said. Since baptism was God's will for every believer, then he ought to be thinking about it himself, shouldn't he? Maybe when things were back to normal and he was back in his new house in town, he'd look at some more Bible references and think about it then.

"Vinnie told me about Caleb."

Uncle Matt leaned back in his seat and ran a hand through his hair. "I knew it was coming. Caleb is a nice lad, but I'd rather they would wait a few years."

"I wasn't sure about his motives for asking her."

"Me neither. It seemed as if he was being motivated by jealousy, asking when he did. Another reason I wasn't happy."

"I think Vinnie is quite relieved, to be honest."

Uncle Matt nodded. "Caleb isn't too happy, though. He's hardly spoken to me since."

Really? Seb couldn't believe that Caleb could hold a grudge like this. He was glad that he was at least speaking to Lavinia, but he knew things were definitely strained between them, lacking the easy camaraderie they had a week ago.

"Anyway, that's between you and me. He'll get over it, I'm sure."

Seb hoped so. He didn't like this side to Caleb and hoped he'd soon get back to normal. He wasn't entirely sure if Caleb was a believer or not, but thought that, if Caleb was a Christian, he shouldn't be interested in Lavinia, who wasn't saved. He'd heard a message back in Belfast about a verse which instructed believers not to be unequally yoked together with unbelievers. The speaker had explained it as two oxen in the olden days yoked together and pulling a plough or some other farming implement. The oxen had to be matched, for if they pulled in different directions, it would be a disaster. He'd pointed out that if a believer and unbeliever were linked together – not only as a couple, maybe even in business – it could end in disaster as they pulled in different directions, with different goals and priorities. Though if Caleb was a Christian who was away from the Lord, he wouldn't be very worried about an unequal yoke.

"Vinnie's finding things really tough, isn't she?" Seb commented.

Uncle Matt looked sad. "She's struggling, Seb. There's a lot going on in her life right now, and she's dealing with it all on her own. We know our Father has everything under control, and we know how to rely on Him, to trust Him. Vinnie has never even trusted Him for her soul's salvation, never mind the little details of life."

"I pray for her a lot, Uncle Matt."

"So do I, Seb. So do I." He looked thoughtful. "I have a feeling that we need to keep praying for her, even more than normal. In fact, why don't we take a few minutes right now to pray for her? Tough times can make us sit up and take note of God's voice, but the devil can also use tough times to cast doubt on God's goodness."

Seb nodded. He had to admit that, during the past few weeks, he had wondered why God let certain things happen – Uncle Matt's accident, the problem between Caleb and Lavinia, the TB reactors. "The devil is still whispering 'Has God said?', like he said to Eve, isn't he?"

"That's right, Seb. And I fear that this is what he's doing with our Vinnie. I'd hate to see these trials, which could well be permitted by God to show her how much she needs Him, become what she uses as an excuse to reject Him."

Seb closed his eyes as Uncle Matt began to pray. The thought of Lavinia rejecting God and never being in heaven was unbearable. No matter how busy life was, he resolved to pray more for his cousin.

For above all the other needs which pressed in on them, the need of her soul was right at the top of the list.

Chapter Fourteen

"So that's where it went." Seb reached under the bedside table, hand flat, and worked the pen free – the one which had gone missing the night Uncle Matt had come home from hospital. He sat back on his heels and surveyed the room. His belongings seemed to have multiplied in the few weeks he'd been staying at Cherryhill, so Aunt Karen had let him borrow a suitcase to take everything back to the little bungalow on the outskirts of town. It was now packed and sitting by the door and Seb was taking a last look for anything he might have missed. Lavinia had been right – the room was a mess. It had taken him ages to gather everything up, but Dale was arriving tomorrow and Aunt Karen needed to clean the room. Tonight, Seb was going back to live with Mum.

"Look at this room!" Lavinia's voice came from the doorway. "It looks so different without all your junk."

Seb pushed himself to his feet. "It's not junk," he replied indignantly.

His cousin smirked at him. "I'm sure Dale will be much neater than you anyway."

"But not as good company."

Lavinia snorted. "Mum's going to take you home once she gets Martha to bed. She wanted me to find out if you're ready to go."

Seb lifted his schoolbag and grabbed the handle of the suitcase. He glanced around the room once more, then flicked off the light.

Uncle Matt was lying on the sofa, his leg propped up on a couple of cushions. He looked up as Seb came through the door. "Got everything packed up?"

"I hope so."

"You'll still come and help out, won't you?" Lavinia flopped into the rocking chair beside the fireplace. "There are still loads of cows to calve, and Dale and I can't do everything."

"Tommy says he's still happy to help out with the evening milking on Mondays and Thursdays," Uncle Matt said. "And Caleb is still coming to help in the mornings."

"Actually," Lavinia said, "Caleb told me that he wants to cut down a bit. He said something about three mornings a week instead of five."

Uncle Matt looked thoughtful. "I'd hoped you would get your mornings back, Vinnie, but if that's the case, then you'll have to do two mornings. I wonder if Caleb would do Tuesdays, Wednesdays and Fridays, so you wouldn't have to do the milking twice in one day."

"Dale will need a bit of time off too." Seb set his luggage down and sat on the arm of Vinnie's chair.

"That's true, Seb. It looks like your help will still be needed a couple of afternoons and maybe at the weekends."

"That's fine." Seb was glad he was still needed. He loved Cherryhill and he couldn't imagine not being there.

The door from the front hallway opened. "Sorry about the wait, Seb. Martha chose a really long story tonight. I tried to condense it, but I was thoroughly reprimanded." Aunt Karen's eyes were laughing. "That's the problem with favourite books. She knows them off by heart and even corrects my mistakes."

Seb stood and lifted the suitcase and his schoolbag. "Thanks for keeping me."

"It was our pleasure. You know you can treat Cherryhill as a second home. We love having you here." Aunt Karen turned to smile at her nephew as she walked across the kitchen and lifted her car keys from the bench.

Uncle Matt adjusted the cushion at his head. "Seb, why don't you take a day or two to get caught up on your schoolwork. I'll be in touch very soon."

Seb waved a hand in farewell and followed Aunt Karen out the door. He was looking forward to a full night's sleep with no need to get up to check on calving cows. He'd have to remember to change the alarm on his phone from 5:15am. He made a quick mental calculation as he lifted the case into the boot. It felt like luxury – two whole hours of a lie in!

———

Seb's eyes flew open. Where was he? What time was it? Had he overslept? Surely Lavinia would be banging on his door if he had. He reached for his phone and his hand whacked against the wall. Huh? Where was the bedside table?

Blinking, he sat up and peered around the gloomy room. Slowly, his senses awakened and with them a dawning realisation that he wasn't at Cherryhill. Instead, he was in his own bedroom at his new house. He reached to the other side and lifted his phone from the light oak bedside table. 6:13. So, he'd had a lie in after all. He smiled wryly. An hour. He lay back and snuggled down under the heavy quilt. It felt strange not having to leap out of bed and quickly change before racing off to help with the milking and feeding. Lately, he'd felt as if he'd been trying to squeeze forty-eight hours into twenty-four.

He closed his eyes and tried to let himself relax, hoping he'd drift off to sleep again. Five minutes later, he knew that wasn't going to happen. He might as well get caught up on some homework. Or some Bible study. He pulled the curtains aside and peeked out. Still dark. He turned on the desk lamp and lifted his Bible from the top of the pile of books, where he'd left it the night before. He flipped through the pages and began to read.

By the time he heard the bathroom door creak, Seb had read through a number of chapters in the book of Acts, spent time in prayer and then finished his geography assignment. He still had a long way to go in catching up on his schoolwork, but at least he was making some progress. He stretched and stood up, then padded to the kitchen in search of breakfast.

"My, you're up early!" Mum stood in the doorway, dressed in her uniform with her hair wrapped in a towel.

"I've been up for over an hour." Seb worked his way along the kitchen cupboards, opening and closing doors.

"If you're looking for cereal, it's in the far cupboard, above the fridge."

"Thanks."

"I'll join you in a few minutes after I've blow-dried my hair."

Seb pulled out the different varieties of cereal and set them on the table. Mum had been busy since he was last here. The freshly-painted red chairs with cream and beige cushions looked suspiciously like the old worn wooden chairs in their last house, and a red-and-cream spotted tablecloth toned in with the framed Bible verse above the table. 'The Son of God, who loved me and gave Himself for me' was spelled out in red letters on a cream background. A red flower decorated one corner and a deep beige surround framed the verse.

Even the dinner set was different. Seb found the bowls and mugs in a cupboard above the kettle, and pulled a couple of spoons from the drawer beside the sink.

"That's better." Mum ran her fingers through her hair as she came into the kitchen. "If I don't dry it in time, it goes all frizzy on me." She gestured to the table. "You found everything, I see."

"Is this set new?" Seb lifted a beige mug.

"New to us." Mum filled the kettle and flipped the switch. "I found a second-hand shop down the street from my work. The whole set was a great price and I knew it would look good with the colour scheme."

"I like the verse."

"Guess who sent that."

Seb shrugged. "I've no idea. Not Aunt Karen?"

"Mrs Thompson! She wanted to give us something for the new house. It arrived in the post last week. I really love the verse, and she didn't know the colour scheme, but she couldn't have done any better if she'd known!"

"Do you think she would come for a visit sometime?" Seb lifted the container of milk from the fridge and filled one of the mugs.

"I hope so."

"She was a great neighbour to have," Seb said wistfully. He didn't miss much about Belfast, but he had been very fond of the old lady.

"I got another letter from your dad's prison the other day."

"Uh-huh?" Seb contemplated the selection of cereal, finally choosing a granola with chunks of chocolate.

"He's still requesting a visit from me." She paused. "I was thinking about it…"

"What?" Seb's hand shook and the granola scattered across the table. Why was Mum so concerned about that man? He had made her life pure misery when she'd lived with him, and had left her with serious injuries. Seb scooped up the pieces of cereal and dumped them into his bowl. "I thought you'd decided not to go." He glanced up at Mum worriedly.

"Well, I was still praying about it, but I don't think it's wise for me to go." The kettle clicked off and Mum carried her mug over to fill it with hot water.

"You're right about that," Seb muttered, toying with his spoon.

"I was also praying about withdrawing the complaint, but I've decided not to withdraw it after all. I think he needs help with his issues."

"That's an understatement," Seb said under his breath.

"The thing is," Mum went on, dropping a tea bag into the mug and pulling a teaspoon from the drawer. She absentmindedly stirred the tea. "He's requested a visit from you again too."

"Mum, no!" Seb dropped the spoon on the table. "I told you I couldn't do it. I can't handle the thought of seeing that man again."

Mum gave him a sympathetic smile. "Seb, I know you struggle with the fact that he's your father, but he is. And more than that, he is a precious soul and God loves him. We are to love our enemies, remember?" She fished the teabag out of the mug and dumped it in the bin under the sink.

Seb sighed. He knew that Mum was right. But Dad? To say that the man had been a horrible father was putting it exceptionally mildly. Seb knew that Dad didn't love him, that, to him, he was nothing but a nuisance, a spineless little kid. And in Dad's eyes, the very worst thing that Seb could do was exactly what had happened during the summer on his first visit to Cherryhill. Seb had become a Christian!

"God might love Dad, but Dad certainly doesn't love God."

Mum slid into the seat opposite and lifted a box of red berry flakes. "All the more reason to show him God's love." She tipped some cereal into her bowl. "But I'm not pushing you, Seb. I know we've already discussed it. And I know how tough he made life for you. He has left both of us with scars – some outward ones for me, and many inward ones for us both. All I'm asking you to do is pray for him. And don't rule out a visit. I'm guessing he'll be there for quite a while."

Seb stirred his cereal around the bowl. He knew that the Bible said that God desires all men to be saved and to come to the knowledge of the truth. But Dad didn't even believe God existed. He hated the very mention of God's name, and thought Christians were people to be despised and mocked. Seb had no idea why Dad was so vicious against anything to do with Christianity. But whatever it was that had caused him to become like this had ingrained itself so deeply into Dad's being that the thought of him ever being saved was – *well, nothing is impossible with God*, thought Seb, *but it certainly would be one of the biggest miracles this world has ever seen.*

Chapter Fifteen

"Did Dale arrive?" Seb spoke over his shoulder as he pulled his books out of his locker.

"Yes, he was there when I got home from school yesterday." Lavinia adjusted her schoolbag on her shoulder and frowned. "He said that our farm was quaint compared to the unit he works on in New Zealand."

"But didn't Uncle Matt put in a new parlour not that long ago?"

"Only last year. I guess even big farms here are on a much smaller scale than out there."

Seb closed the locker and shoved the books into his bag. "I'd love to go there to work. Maybe I should take a gap year sometime."

"You can speak to Dale. Maybe he could get you some work on the dairy farm where he works."

Seb fell into step beside his cousin as they made their way to maths. "So apart from calling Cherryhill quaint, how is he to work with?"

Lavinia shrugged. "Tommy was helping him with the milking yesterday, but as far as I could tell Dale seems to know what he's doing and is friendly enough. You'll see for yourself when you're next there. Was Dad in touch about which days you're helping with milking?"

Seb nodded. "He phoned last night. He needs me Wednesdays and Fridays, so I'm getting the bus home with you this afternoon."

"Good. I wasn't sure what he was going to organise. Even with Dale there, there's still so much to do, especially with the cows calving."

They entered the classroom. Seb made his way to the back, to where Danny was sitting with his phone. As he sat down, he glanced up and noticed Lavinia bypassing the free seat beside Rebekah and sitting beside Jasmine instead. He frowned. Why was she ignoring Rebekah these days? He knew that things weren't too good between her and Caleb, but Rebekah had been Lavinia's friend since they were babies. Should he go and talk to Rebekah? He half rose from his seat.

"Okay, class," Mrs Craig entered the room. "Quieten down."

Seb sank back down. He'd missed his chance. Maybe he'd get an opportunity to talk to Rebekah later.

Seb's opportunity didn't come until later that day. Lavinia had headed off somewhere at lunchtime with Jasmine, and Seb spotted Rebekah sitting quietly reading in a corner of the classroom by herself. She looked up as he joined her, and set her book aside.

"What are you reading?"

She lifted the book to let him see the cover. "*Through Gates of Splendour*. It's a biography about Jim Elliot and the other missionaries who were killed in Ecuador by a tribe that they were hoping to share the gospel with. It's really good."

Seb reached for the book and read the back cover. "It looks good. Maybe I could borrow it sometime." He laughed. "After I get caught up on all my homework and don't have to help out so much at Cherryhill."

Rebekah smiled. "Of course. How are things at the farm these days?"

"It's been hard. At least Dale is there now, but between Uncle Matt's accident and the TB test, it hasn't been a great time."

"And this problem between Vinnie and Caleb..." Rebekah looked at Seb hesitantly.

"You know about it?"

"I knew something was wrong. Caleb has been acting a bit like that bull that attacked Matt. You just don't want to get in his way. He finally told me."

"Vinnie isn't coping too well either."

Rebekah sighed. "I noticed. I'm not sure why she's avoiding me, but she hardly speaks to me these days. I mean, it's not my fault that Caleb tried to bully her into being his girlfriend."

Seb gave a wry laugh. "That's exactly what he was doing."

"Maybe I remind her of happier times, when things were a bit less complicated. Or she thinks that I approve of Caleb's behaviour."

"I'm sure she knows what you think." Seb knew that Rebekah and her older brother were very close, but also knew that she wasn't afraid to keep Caleb right if the situation demanded it.

"I just don't know why it was all so urgent that he had to ask her now, when things are really stressful at Cherryhill, instead of waiting until the summer, when everything will hopefully have calmed down a bit and Vinnie's exams will be over."

"Uncle Matt might have been happier about it by then," agreed Seb. "But it was really to do with Diarmuid."

"Diarmuid?" Rebekah looked blank. "Oh! The vet that Vinnie says has a gorgeous accent?"

"That's the one." He rolled his eyes and Rebekah giggled. "Caleb's nose got a little out of joint the day of the TB test. Especially since she decided to stay chatting to Diarmuid rather than join Caleb when he was doing the milking."

Rebekah winced. "No wonder Caleb's a bit grumpy these days. He always had a bit of a problem with being possessive. Oldest child syndrome and all that."

"Huh?"

"Not finding it easy to share. Also typical of people who are an only child." Her blue eyes twinkled and she put a hand up to cover a smile.

"Hey!" He laughed, taken aback by her unexpected teasing.

"Well, this is cosy." A shadow fell across the desk.

Rebekah looked up. "Hi, Danny. Pull over a seat."

"Naw. I need to go and hand in an essay. It's late as it is." He shot a glare at Seb and left the room.

"What was all that about?" Rebekah looked mystified.

Seb grinned. "Where does Danny come in his family?"

"He has one younger sister, but what does that... Oh!" She looked down and bit her lip. A faint blush rose on her cheeks.

Taking pity on his friend, he decided it was time to change the subject. "So what do you make of Vinnie being so friendly with Jasmine?"

Rebekah toyed with the spine of her book. "Honestly, Seb? Jasmine was my science partner last year and I really like her, but I fear she's trying to influence Vinnie against the Christian upbringing she's had. I already heard her ask Vinnie why she needed to go to church every week. Jasmine thinks that God doesn't need our church attendance to show whether we're good people or not."

Seb sighed. "And there is a little bit of truth in that. Going to church doesn't make us Christians, but it's the place where people should hear that the Lord Jesus Christ died so that sinners can be forgiven."

"I hope she doesn't try to get out of going." Rebekah looked at Seb in concern. "I think she's pulling away from what she's been taught."

Seb nodded slowly. "You're right. She's said a few things lately that worry me, to be honest."

"We need to pray for her more than ever, Seb. I'd hate to see her reject the truth." Tears stood in Rebekah's blue eyes. Her words were an echo of Seb's thoughts of the other night. He was glad to have a fellow believer join in praying for Lavinia's soul, to battle the forces of darkness who were determined to keep his cousin from salvation until it was too late.

"I am so glad it's Friday afternoon." Lavinia adjusted her schoolbag on her shoulder as she stepped off the bus.

"Are you going to try to catch up with your homework this weekend?" Seb followed close behind.

She snorted. "Catching up isn't possible, but I'll maybe get a little bit more done."

"I'm not looking forward to that English essay. It's going to take ages to research and write."

Lavinia tossed her head. "Not today's problem."

The bus pulled away, and Seb coughed at the cloud of exhaust fumes. They crossed the road and began walking up the slight incline of the lane. Seb startled as he heard Lavinia groan.

"What is it?"

She pointed to the end of the lane. "They were supposed to come earlier today. I hoped they'd be gone before we got back from school."

Seb frowned. A cattle lorry was parked in the yard, the ramp lowered. A dawning realisation spread cold dread through him. The

TB reactors. Today was the day that they were to be taken away. To be culled.

Uncle Matt stood to one side, leaning on his crutches, face sombre. Seb and Lavinia moved towards him and stood one on either side. He looked first at Lavinia, then at Seb, and gave an attempt at a smile. "I'm sorry. I'd hoped they'd be here sooner."

"So did I." Lavinia heaved a great sigh, her lower lip trembling.

Uncle Matt lifted a hand off his crutch and wobbled as he put his arm around his daughter's shoulders. "Why don't you go into the house? You don't need to watch."

"Now that I'm here, I can't not watch."

Matt gave her shoulder a squeeze. Seb figured that they all felt the same way. Just then, the clatter of hooves sounded in the shed and cattle made their way into the yard. They paused, eyes wide. Some sniffed the air, others bawled. Lavinia's heifer looked directly towards where they were standing.

"Oh, Dad," Seb heard Lavinia whimper.

"I know, Vinnie. I know." Uncle Matt's voice sounded husky, as if he were close to tears.

"Look at her. So beautiful. She would've made champion at next year's show. I just know it." Lavinia buried her head in her dad's chest. Seb could hear her muffled sobs.

Dale and the driver steered the cattle towards the lorry and they tramped up the ramp. Eighteen reactors, two inconclusives. Twenty expensive, well-bred, much-cared-for cattle. Most of them had passed through the parlour twice a day. Seb had milked them, each time appreciating their docile ways, their impressive frames, their glossy coats and their gentle eyes. He stole a glance at Uncle Matt. It would be harder for him. Uncle Matt knew each cow individually. Her temperament, her yield, her bloodline, how many calves she'd had. And then there were those still to calve, whose calves, yet in the womb, would never see the light of day, never become full-fledged dairy cows, never pass on the valuable genes, but would perish with their mothers.

All because of two dread-filled letters. TB.

The driver closed the doors and made his way to Uncle Matt. "That's them loaded up, Matt. If you could just sign here." He held out a clipboard and pointed to a spot with a pen.

Uncle Matt lifted his arm from Lavinia's shoulder and reached for the pen. "If you hold the clipboard, Darren, I'll sign it."

Lavinia pulled away and wiped her eyes with a sodden tissue. Her face was blotchy and her eyes were red.

"Sure thing." The driver braced the clipboard and Matt squiggled his signature on the page. "You've had a run of bad luck, Matt. Hope things will soon look up for you."

Matt handed the pen back. "I hope so. Although I'm not sure I'd call it luck all the same. God knows what He's doing."

Darren looked at him sceptically. "He's not being very kind to you."

Matt smiled. "That's where you're wrong, Darren. Someone who gives His Son to die for me is, well, kind is a bit of an understatement, I'd say. These other things," he waved his hand towards his leg, then to the lorry, "God has a purpose for them. He doesn't make mistakes."

Darren grunted. "Well, I'd better get going, Matt. All the best."

Uncle Matt waved a hand as the man made his way to the lorry and climbed into the driver's seat. As the lorry started up, Seb could hear the cattle shifting around. They didn't know what was happening, or why.

Dale came over to join them as the lorry made its way down the lane. "Shame for those cattle to have to go," he said. "You've built up an impressive herd over the years, Matt, and there were a lot of good cows there."

No one spoke as the lorry slowed before turning out onto the road. It disappeared from sight and gradually the roar of the diesel engine faded into the distance.

It was gone. Seb swallowed down a lump in his throat.

Within a matter of hours, twenty of Uncle Matt's best cows would be dead.

Chapter Sixteen

Seb squinted against the brightness of the low winter sun. The November morning was clear, with brilliant blue skies and even a touch of frost on the lawns of the neat bungalows of the cul-de-sac. He breathed in the crisp air and hoisted his schoolbag a little higher on his shoulder as he walked. While he missed the camaraderie on the bus from Cherryhill to school, he enjoyed the walk from home. This was a quiet, peaceful area, right on the outskirts of the town and nothing at all like the busy bustle of Belfast. It was hard not to appreciate his surroundings, especially on a morning like this.

Seb walked past the prim and proper corner house and turned left onto a larger street. Leaves from the tall trees above him lay on the ground, their lines and ridges marked with white frost. Leaves really did have such a short lifespan. Only a few months, then they fell and decomposed. Yet even in their decomposition, they provided nutrients for another generation. A bit like those old missionaries and godly believers who died years ago, yet books about them inspired young people to live for God.

Life was short, there was no doubt about that. And Seb was sure that he wanted to make his life count. Was there something that he could be doing for God that he hadn't thought of? He tried to make use of any opportunities that arose at school, to be helpful in any way he could, and to speak to others about the Lord Jesus, but was there something else?

He looked both ways and crossed the road. He'd been reading in the Bible about Paul that morning, how he had shared the gospel whenever he could, even to Roman rulers and Gentile kings. *Probably scary people*, Seb thought. People who had the power to kill him if they so desired. Some listened, but some mocked what he had to say. Yet he still continued to witness for God.

Seb clenched his jaw as a thought bubbled up in his conscience. No, God. Please, not him. Seb would nearly rather go and speak to a Roman ruler. Yet Dad needed to hear the gospel too. And now, with him in prison, maybe he'd have more time to think of such things. Seb's legs trembled at the thought of seeing his father again. Would God really ask him to go and visit the monster who had terrorised him, mocked him, humiliated him through most of his life? Did God really expect Seb to go and show him love? The man who had never shown love to his wife or son? The man who didn't seem to have the first clue as to what love was?

Unbidden, words forced their way into Seb's mind. *Go into all the world and preach the gospel to every creature.*

Every creature. Including Dad.

Seb took a shaky breath. “Okay, God. I’ll go.” He didn’t expect to enjoy it. He didn’t expect that Dad would even listen. In fact, he was pretty sure that, after this visit, Dad would refuse to see him ever again.

But Seb would go. In fear and trembling, and in dependence on God.

Because Mum was right. God did love Dad. He loved him so much that He gave His only Son. And whether Dad even believed there was a God or not didn’t change the great fact that God loved him.

“I’ve decided to visit Dad.” Seb plopped down in the seat across the table from Rebekah.

She looked up from her book and smiled. “Good for you! That’s going to take some courage.”

Seb’s stomach clenched. “You’re dead right. I’m totally dreading it.” He’d already told her about Mum’s idea and his reluctance to see his father again.

She lifted a purple-tasselled bookmark and dropped it into the book, then set it aside. “From what you’ve told me, I can understand why.”

“Yeah, he hasn’t exactly been a wonderful father.”

“So do you know when his trial is?”

“Not yet, but it won’t be long. Mum was talking to Dad’s lawyer, or was it a solicitor...?" He squinted as he tried to remember the correct term, then shrugged. "One of those legal people anyway. He expects it'll be within the next couple of months."

"Are you planning to be there?" Rebekah leaned her elbows on the desk and rested her chin in her hands.

Seb smiled. "To be honest, my plan was to stay as far away from Dad for as long as I could get away with it! God just changed that, so who knows?"

"Is your mum going to the trial?"

"I haven't asked her, but I have a feeling she'll want to be there. I'm not sure why, exactly. It won't be easy, especially for her."

"Maybe she feels a sort of duty to him. I mean, she's still married to him, isn't she?"

"She's never mentioned getting a divorce." He sighed. "What I'm really worried about is that when he gets out of prison he'll sweet talk her into taking him back and she'll be right back to the life she's escaped."

"Or," Rebekah lifted an eyebrow, "he'll get saved and things will be better than they've ever been for them."

For a moment, he allowed himself to dream. What would it be like if Dad was saved and they were a normal family unit? Reading the Bible at breakfast together, praying, discussing passages of Scripture with Dad... No, he couldn't imagine it. The very idea of Dad holding a Bible was ludicrous. He sighed. "I wish I had your faith, Rebekah."

"Don't forget that all things are possible with God. That's what I'm praying for anyway." She gave him a shy smile. "And I'll be praying that God will give you the right words when you go to visit him."

Seb smiled back. Maybe, with Rebekah's prayers and God's help, he could do this after all. Once more, he silently thanked God for giving him a friend like Rebekah.

"Mm. Mum's been baking."

The smell of freshly-baked scones greeted Seb and Lavinia at the door. Uncle Matt and Dale sat at the table, Uncle Matt with a lever arch file opened in front of him and his leg propped on a chair. Dale was dressed in casual clothes, and was reading a sheet of paper that looked like it was from Uncle Matt's file.

"Vinnie, look at my picture." Martha leaped off her chair and waved a page in the air. "It's Glen and Jess." She pointed to two black shapes on the page.

"Who's this?" Lavinia indicated the pink blob in the centre.

Martha frowned. "It's me. You should know that, Vinnie. You mustn't be very smart after all."

"Whoever said I was smart to begin with?" Lavinia replied breezily as she plonked herself down in the chair across from Dale.

Dale looked up and smiled at her. "How was school today?"

"It was okay," she replied. "I just wish they'd give us less homework."

Seb shed his blazer and pulled out the chair next to Lavinia.

Dale's gaze moved to Seb. "And you, Seb? How did you find it?"

"Fine. I much prefer this school to my last one."

"You knew Seb recently moved from Belfast?" asked Aunt Karen, as she spread jam onto the scones and finished them with a blob of fresh cream. "Seb and his mum live in a house on the outskirts of town."

"And your dad?" asked Dale mildly.

"He's–" Seb swallowed. He really didn't want to tell a virtual stranger the truth. Having a father in prison, awaiting trial for drug smuggling charges, wasn't something he enjoyed talking about. "He's not with us. My parents are separated."

"That's too bad."

Seb refrained from telling him that it wasn't too bad. That his parents' separation had come as a huge relief to him. That he really wasn't keen on seeing his father again.

"Seb stayed with us during the summer for the first time. He'd hardly ever been out of Belfast, but he took to farming like no one I've ever seen. He's a natural." Uncle Matt smiled at Seb.

Seb toyed with the handle of the mug. He'd hardly call himself a natural, but he couldn't deny he loved the farm.

"Do you hope to do something farming related when you leave school?" Dale set the page he'd been looking at to one side.

"I'd like to. Maybe do an agriculture-related degree at university."

"He told me he'd like to take a gap year and maybe work on a dairy unit in New Zealand," Lavinia said.

Seb looked down self-consciously. He had wondered about bringing the subject around with Dale sometime, but hadn't thought of telling him so soon.

"Great idea," Dale said, his smile making him look even more like Uncle Matt. "I happen to know of a good dairy unit that might give you some work."

Lavinia grinned and nudged Seb. Whatever she'd been about to say was cut off by the shrill ring of the house phone. Aunt Karen wiped her hands on her apron and lifted it off the bench.

"Hello? Yes, sure. One moment." She lowered her voice as she handed the phone to Matt. "It's Derek from Pasture Dairies."

Uncle Matt took the phone. "Hello, Derek... Yes, we're well... Coming on, slow progress, but I'll get there... Thanks, I appreciate that..." He frowned, then began to swing his injured leg off the other chair. "Repeat that, Derek..." He ran his fingers through his hair. "I've no idea... I'll have to ask and see... Yes, we've quite a few different workers at the minute..."

Seb glanced at Lavinia. What was going on? She was leaning forwards, watching her dad intently.

"I understand, Derek... Yes, I know that's the way it works... Don't worry, we'll not let it happen again... Okay, bye for now." Uncle Matt blew out a puff of air and dropped the phone onto the table.

Everyone had frozen in place. The daub of cream on Aunt Karen's spoon splatted onto the floor, but she didn't seem to notice.

"That was Derek from the dairy. They've discovered that the load in the milk tanker that called here this morning was contaminated with antibiotics, and," he shook his head in disbelief, "he says it was traced to Cherryhill Farm."

Chapter Seventeen

"But, Dad, since we started to use teat sealants, we have very few cows on antibiotics now." Lavinia's eyes were wide. "And everyone knows to dump the milk from those cows."

Uncle Matt suddenly looked old and weary. "I know that, Vinnie, but we're going to have to check with everyone that the milk was dumped and that no one administered any antibiotics for any reason and forgot to mark the cow."

Seb knew that Uncle Matt used a system of marking any cows that had received antibiotics with coloured tape on their tails. This meant that anyone doing the milking could see that the cow had been treated with antibiotics and therefore knew to discard the milk until the appropriate withdrawal period had passed.

"What's going to happen now?" asked Seb. He didn't know much about the testing procedures at the dairy, but he was pretty sure that antibiotics in the milk was a serious matter.

"They have to dump the whole tankerload of milk because it will have contaminated the rest of the load. It could be in the region of twenty-five to thirty thousand litres, so it's a lot of milk."

"Which we have to pay for," Lavinia said flatly.

"How much will that cost?"

"We're talking quite a few thousand pounds. We won't get paid for our own milk either." Uncle Matt rubbed a hand down his cheek.

"Does your insurance cover you for this, Matt?" Dale asked. His eyes had narrowed and he seemed concerned for his cousin.

"I hope so, Dale. Things are going to be a bit tight before we get the payment, and the compensation for the TB reactors won't happen overnight either, not to mention the loss of income from the unborn calves of some of those reactors." Uncle Matt didn't mention Dale's wages or the money he paid Caleb to work on the farm. He'd tried to give Seb a regular wage too, but Seb had insisted that he was family and didn't need anything. It hadn't stopped Uncle Matt from slipping him an occasional banknote now and again.

Uncle Matt cleared his throat. "Dale, I hate to ask, but you'll understand I need assurances from everyone who has access to the cows. You didn't happen to administer any antibiotics since you arrived?"

Dale's eyes flew open. "Certainly not, Matt! I feel very strongly about the unnecessary use of antibiotics. And I'm certain I discarded the milk from the cows on antibiotics."

Matt nodded. "Thanks, Dale. I'm of the same opinion on unnecessary antibiotics." He turned to his nephew. "Seb, I don't need to ask you. The milk was last lifted on Monday morning, and you haven't been here since then."

"I wouldn't know how to inject a cow anyway."

"Well, Tommy was here on Monday evening, and Caleb yesterday morning, so you'll need to check with them," Lavinia commented. "I definitely dumped the antibiotic milk and I didn't go near the antibiotics either."

Aunt Karen set the plate of scones on the table and lifted the teapot from the Aga's hotplate. Lavinia put milk in each mug and Karen filled them up with tea.

Uncle Matt gave thanks for the food and they made short work of the scones. Seb went to the bathroom to change his clothes and then followed Dale out to the parlour. Jess lifted her head and growled as Dale walked past, but didn't bother to follow.

"I had forgotten what it was like to work on a small farm," Dale remarked as he started up the milking machine and put a milking apron over his head.

"Vinnie says that this is a large farm by Northern Irish standards."

Dale chuckled. "That may be so, but this is nothing compared to New Zealand. You'll have to come and see it for yourself. Maybe get the bug and stay on, like me."

"Did you intend to stay for so long?" Seb lifted disposable gloves out of the box and pulled them on.

"I planned to go for a year, but I guess I fell in love with the place. I enjoy living there." Dale let the first row of cows into the parlour. The black and white animals moved slowly up the row and Dale prodded their rumps to manoeuvre them into position.

"Would you want to come back and live here?" Seb pulled off a length of blue roll and began to wipe the cows' teats.

"What would I come back for? Dairying is all I know, but buying a farm is well outside my budget and being a farmhand here is a different story to helping manage a large herd out there."

"Doesn't your sister miss you?"

Dale gave a guffaw of laughter. "Clarissa? She's an artist and all wrapped up in her own world. She made it very clear that I was in her way. She gave me a real dressing down for tracking mud into her house. But really, who in their right mind has a pure white carpet in the hallway? And there was nothing in the house to eat! Raw vegetables, nuts and seeds. She went pale when I suggested cooking steak."

Seb smiled. "Is she vegetarian?"

"Worse. Vegan. She told me she 'deeply disapproves' of my choice of career, that it's unfair to keep cows for their milk, and to take the 'baby cows', as she called them, away from their mothers."

"Didn't she spend time here when she was young, the way you did?"

"She always hated the farm. Mum dragged her here on occasions to visit Uncle George, but she sat primly in the corner with her toes tucked under her chair and a pained expression on her face."

Seb laughed when Dale pursed his lips delicately and frowned in an imitation of his sister. "So you don't really miss her, then."

“Not really. My dad died when we were quite young, and my mum passed away after a heart attack just before I left for New Zealand. So there’s nothing really to come back to.”

“Why did you decide to visit? To see Clarissa?”

Dale snorted. “Well, that seemed like a good idea when I was booking my flights. I don’t think she was worrying about me anyway.” He let the second row of cows into the parlour and began to wipe them down.

“How many years is it since you last saw Uncle Matt?”

Dale gazed towards the parlour door, deep in thought. “I was home for a family wedding shortly before Matt graduated. That was just after Uncle George died.” He looked back towards the cows. An almost imperceptible flicker passed across the man’s face. Not quite sadness, but similar.

He must have been very close to his Uncle George, Seb thought. “You probably wanted to catch up with Uncle Matt again and see all the places you used to know when you were young.”

Dale blinked. “Huh? Yes, yes. That’s right. This is a very scenic part of the world. Not like some of the lakes and mountains of New Zealand, of course, but I suppose the place where you grow up will always be a special spot.”

Seb frowned. He really didn’t consider Belfast very special. The memories he had were anything but pleasant. “I think I prefer Cherryhill Farm to where I grew up.”

"You really like this place, don't you?" Dale seemed to be staring intently at him.

Seb nodded. "This is the place where I first learned that there is a God after all, and that He loves me."

"You didn't know about God?"

"Oh, I knew about God, but I didn't think He existed. After I came to Cherryhill, I opened my eyes and began to see all the evidence for a Creator. And then I learned that God gave His Son to die for my sins, and one evening I trusted Him. I'm a Christian now."

Dale turned back towards the cows and grunted.

"Are you a Christian, Dale?"

Dale was silent as he removed the clusters from the cow. Finally, "No, I couldn't say that I am."

"Do you believe there's a God?"

The man threw a shoulder upwards in a shrug. "I guess so. I haven't really thought much about it one way or the other."

"But you know–"

"Seb, let's just leave this topic of conversation, okay? I'd rather not talk about such matters." Dale's eyes had narrowed and his mouth was set in a hard line.

Seb sighed. Maybe he'd be better leaving all mention of God for now. *Another person to add to my prayer list*, he thought.

"So how do you think the antibiotics got into the milk?" Dale changed the subject.

"I have no idea. Do you think the dairy got it wrong? Maybe it was some other farm's milk."

"I don't think so. They're usually pretty careful with the individual farm samples. There are other things that they check for, maybe butterfat or protein, that should be fairly consistent from one time to the next, which would help them identify it if it had got mixed up."

Seb sprayed the cows with disinfectant spray and let them out of the parlour. He really had no idea what had happened or how the antibiotics had got into the milk.

"Maybe Tommy or Caleb can shed some light on it. They might have given antibiotics and forgotten to mark the cow."

"If either of them made a mistake like that, they'd need to be strongly reprimanded. It's not an inconsequential error."

Seb blinked. Dale hadn't struck him as the type to use such formal language. "Do you think one of them did that?"

"Well, I don't know what Tommy's memory is like, but he's been farming for years and I can't see him giving a cow antibiotics without discussing it with Matt first. And Caleb seems clued in when it comes to farming."

"So do you think one of them might have–"

"That boy has a big chip on his shoulder about something," Dale interrupted. "Or maybe that's what he's like all the time. Either way, he sure is a grumpy lad."

"He's not always like that." Seb felt compelled to stand up for

Rebekah's red-haired big brother. "He's usually good fun and I never saw him lose his temper until... " He drifted off, afraid he'd said too much.

"Until when?" Dale pressed.

"I-I can't really say." Dale might be family, but Seb certainly didn't want to tell him about Lavinia's problems.

"So there was a row of some sort, then." Dale looked almost smug. "That would explain a lot. I couldn't work out why Matt kept such a sullen, moody person working for him. I wonder what the row was about... "

Seb concentrated on the nearest cow, carefully wiping away every speck of dirt from the pink teats.

"Nothing so serious that would cause him to conveniently forget to discard antibiotic-contaminated milk, I'm sure." Dale's voice was mildly sarcastic.

Seb whipped around. "Dale, that's ridiculous. Caleb would never do that. He's almost part of the family, he's known them for so long. He'd never purposely set out to jeopardise the farm."

"Hm." Dale's grunt was noncommittal.

Seb moved to the next cow. Dale was wrong. Seb knew it. Caleb might be exceedingly difficult to get on with these days, but Seb knew one thing about him. He was genuine.

Wasn't he?

Chapter Eighteen

"So what happened?" Lavinia flung her hands in the air. "I mean, there has to be some reason for the contamination. Antibiotics just don't end up in milk for no reason."

"I don't know, Vinnie." Matt rubbed a hand through his hair again, which was already standing on end. "Both Caleb and Tommy said they were sure they had discarded the milk that needed to be discarded, and confirmed that they haven't been near the antibiotics, never mind administer them. I can only put it down to a mistake – someone missed seeing the tape on the cow's tail somehow."

Dale cut off a large chunk of mince pie and raised it to his mouth. As he chewed, he looked in Seb's direction and raised an eyebrow, obviously cynical about Caleb's truthfulness.

Seb stabbed a few pieces of carrot with his fork. Surely Caleb wouldn't do anything to harm the farm? He might be disgruntled with Uncle Matt and even Lavinia these days, but he wouldn't go that far. Would he?

And yet, these days he really wasn't acting like the Caleb Seb had known.

Seb lifted his glass and drained the apple juice. He felt bad even entertaining such a thought, but maybe it would do no harm to watch Caleb more closely from now.

Aunt Karen cleared the plates from the table, and Lavinia brought out the meringue roulade.

"Karen, is that raspberry and white chocolate?" Dale rubbed his slightly paunchy mid-section.

"It is indeed, Dale."

"Ah, that's great. My favourite combination." He turned to Matt. "You sure landed on your feet, cousin."

Matt smiled warmly at Karen. "Didn't I just? No word of any romance in your life?"

Dale's smile didn't quite reach his eyes. "What woman would put up with the sort of hours I work?"

"Surely there's some lady out there for you, Dale." Lavinia set a pile of small plates on the table and returned for pastry forks.

"Well, Vinnie, if there is, I haven't met her yet."

"Maybe you'll meet her here in Northern Ireland," Karen said, laughing.

Dale snorted. "Don't any of you be setting me up with someone. You hear?"

Lavinia giggled. "Well, there's always Madge."

"Dear old Madge." Dale slowly shook his head. "Is talking still her favourite hobby?"

"Oh yes!" Lavinia laughed. "It's strange that she hasn't been to see you yet."

"She'll be here in the next day or two." Uncle Matt took his plate of roulade from Aunt Karen. "Maybe Tommy hasn't got round to telling her that you're here. He can be a bit selective in what he tells her, because he knows that particular topic will come up many times in conversation before she'll let it drop. And someone returning here after so many years abroad… Well, that sort of thing excites Madge no end."

"She'll want to ask what New Zealand is like, then she'll tell you about everybody she ever knew who either visited, moved to or lived in New Zealand. She'll probably exclaim over the family likeness to Dad, but then point out how she knows the two of you apart, a bit like a living, breathing spot-the-difference game. And that'll just be her getting started."

Everyone laughed at Lavinia's accurate depiction of Madge.

"Maybe I should make sure I'm out working when she calls."

"Oh no!" Lavinia exclaimed. "You really should meet her again. She's good fun."

"More than that, Vinnie, she's a very generous and kindly lady. She really has what the old folks call 'a heart of corn'."

"I know that, Dad. There's no one like Madge, but you have to admit she can be very entertaining." Lavinia scraped the meringue crumbs and cream from the plate and popped them into her mouth.

"I'm going to go and check the cows." She pushed back her chair. "Coming, Seb?"

Seb looked towards Aunt Karen.

"Go ahead. I'm going to clear up the dishes and then put Martha to bed. I'll leave you home after that."

Seb followed Lavinia out the door. He stopped to change into his wellies and grab a coat from the office. As they walked across the yard, Seb took a deep breath. Mist had fallen and the smell of cows lingered in the chilly, moisture-laden air.

"November is such a dull month," Lavinia sighed.

Seb gave a dry chuckle. "I assume you're talking about the weather, because we're not even halfway through the month and so far it's been anything but dull."

Lavinia blew out a quick breath. "You're certainly not exaggerating about that. Maybe dull would be good after all. I can't remember a time when so many awful things happened, and all at once too." She entered the shed and turned on a light.

"It's certainly hard to understand. Your dad's accident, the dead calf, the TB test, now this problem with the milk."

"And Caleb's attitude," she finished flatly. "Why couldn't he have let things be the way they were? And what awful timing. Does he really think that I have time for a boyfriend right now anyway?" She stopped at a pen and leaned her arms on the gate.

"I think he just got jealous of Diarmuid. Caleb always had your undivided attention and I think he couldn't cope when you pretty much ignored him."

Lavinia flushed and looked away.

"Vinnie… " Should he mention Dale's suspicions? Even though she didn't seem to be as infatuated with Caleb as she had been, Seb didn't want to get on her bad side by accusing the person who had been her almost-boyfriend for so long. She still had feelings for Caleb, Seb was sure of it.

"What is it?" Lavinia was watching him, a puzzled look on her face.

"Oh, nothing. I was just wondering if you had any ideas about who made a mistake with the antibiotics."

She shook her head. "I've been thinking non-stop about that. I mean, everyone who works on the farm knows the protocol, that you dump the milk from those cows that have been treated, and that antibiotics aren't used unless they are really necessary."

"Do you think that it might have been done on purpose?" Seb asked, holding his breath.

"On purpose? Why would someone do that?" She frowned. "*Who* would do that?"

Seb shrugged. "I don't know. Maybe someone with a grudge against your dad. Or against you."

Lavinia swung away from the gate. "Seb, that's ridiculous! Dad doesn't have any enemies. Neither do I."

Seb watched a spider working on a web in the corner of the pen.

"It was just a thought."

Lavinia was silent for a few moments, then – "Seb! Surely you don't think that Caleb did it? Because if that's what you think, that's really unfair. He might be a bit," she paused as if she was casting around in her mind for an appropriate word, "a bit grumpy at the minute, but he'd certainly never do *that*."

Seb bit his lip. He hadn't suggested it, only implied it. And Lavinia's reaction was something similar to what his own had been when Dale had suggested it. Yet, Caleb was the only one who had a motive. Maybe he'd done it on a spur of the moment, unplanned and unpremeditated, and was even now regretting what he'd done.

"That's really judgmental of you, Seb. Jasmine said Christians are judgmental people, and I think she's right."

Woah. *What?* "Vinnie, what are you talking about? I never said Caleb did it. And what else has Jasmine been feeding you?"

"Nothing. It was just something she said one day."

"I thought you and Rebekah were best friends, but you've hardly spoken to her lately."

Lavinia turned back to the gate and began to rub her thumb over the surface of the upper bar. Back and forth. Back and forth. "She's still my friend," she said quietly, "but she likes to talk about God."

"You don't want to hear about God?" He knew Lavinia wasn't a Christian, but she'd always been respectful and reverent.

"He let the bull attack Dad, the calf be born dead, the TB test come back positive, and now this problem with the milk. He could have stopped any of those things from happening. Couldn't He?" She raised her chin defiantly.

Seb nodded. "Yes. Yes, He could have."

"So why didn't He?"

Seb sighed. He really didn't know. In fact, he'd even thought the same thing, had asked God why. "I don't know why, Vinnie. All I know is that the Bible says that God is love and so anything that He permits is done out of love. Maybe some of us need to learn a lesson that can't be taught any other way."

"Well, that's just mean. Why should we all suffer so one person can learn something?"

"Maybe everyone needs to learn something. Maybe one trial will teach different things to everyone who is affected."

"Well, I'm not so sure. You prayed that the TB test would be clear, didn't you? You thought God could work a miracle. But He didn't." She paused. "In fact, maybe He's not even there at all. You were just talking into the air."

"Vinnie!" Seb gasped. "How can you think such a thing? Of course God is there! Don't tell me that you think there is no God!"

She shrugged.

Seb shook his head. Lavinia had been born into and brought up in a Christian home. She'd seen first-hand the peace that comes through faith in God. Seb had grown up with an atheistic father who'd filled his mind with anti-God rhetoric. Seb had swallowed everything he'd been told. It had taken his coming to Cherryhill to open his eyes. But Lavinia, of all people, suddenly doubting God's existence?

"I need to check those cows. Give me two minutes and then we'll go back to the house. Mum will be ready to take you home soon."

He waited at the door of the shed, Lavinia's words rolling around in his mind. He *knew* that God was there, that He was real. He'd experienced His saving grace in his own life. But how could he help his cousin see that even though problems and hard times came, God was still there? Still caring. Still loving.

He heard her footsteps on the concrete behind him and took a breath. He had to say something. "Vinnie, you can't–"

"Seb," she interrupted. " I know what you and Dad and Mum believe, that God has let all these things happen for a reason, but it doesn't make sense to me. I mean, why would God let bad things happen to good people, those who've trusted Him? And what about all the evil in the world – the bad things that people do to each other? He could stop that if He wanted."

She paused and turned to face Seb. In the faint light from across the yard he could see the pain in her face reflecting the anguish of countless millions across the world as they searched for answers to an age-old problem.

"Seb, if there really is a God, why is there so much suffering?"

Chapter Nineteen

Lavinia's question burned a hole in Seb's mind through the rest of the week and into the weekend. Why did God permit so much suffering?

Seb was absolutely certain that God was all-powerful. He was equally sure that God loved the world – John chapter three and verse sixteen said so. *For God so loved the world that He gave His only begotten Son...* So why didn't God put a stop to suffering? Seb knew without a doubt that God is righteous, but he was at a loss as to the answer to Lavinia's question.

"God created man with a free will," the speaker said on Sunday evening. "He gave him the choice of whether to obey, or to disobey. Man chose to disobey. Was God surprised? Taken aback by man's disobedience?" He paused. "No! God knew what Adam would do. He knew he would fail. God's foreknowledge of man's failure doesn't make Him responsible for that failure. He already had a remedy in mind for man's sinfulness. Years later, God would send His own Son to earth to die for the sin of mankind."

If God knew what man would do, why did He create him with a free will? Seb pondered later that evening. *Why not create him without the ability to choose sin?*

Seb stretched out on his bed, hands behind his head, and began to imagine what life would be like without a free will. No ability to sin – to hate, to covet, to worship anyone or anything other than God. Wouldn't that have been ideal? A perfect world. Everyone living in harmony and peace.

A light tap sounded at the door and Mum poked her head in. She smiled when she saw Seb. "Chilling out?" she asked.

"Thinking," he replied. He pushed himself up and rested his back against the headboard, then motioned to the end of the bed. "Come in. I want to ask you something."

Mum entered the room and sat on the edge of the bed. "What is it?" She looked bemused.

"I was thinking about suffering, and evil, and man's free will."

Mum blinked. "Deep thoughts, Seb. I wasn't expecting that!"

"What did you think I wanted to ask you?"

"Oh, I don't know. Something to do with school, or girls, or–"

"Girls?" Seb rolled his eyes, embarrassed. "Why would you think I'd ask..." He shook his head. "Never mind."

"So what's your question?"

"I was wondering why God gave man a free will if He knew that he was going to sin anyway."

Mum nodded slowly and smiled. "You know, I've been thinking

about the same question lately. Especially with the way your dad has treated us. Why didn't God stop him? For that matter, why didn't God stop me from ever leaving home and getting into that situation? Why did He give us the choice of obeying or disobeying Him?"

Seb adjusted the pillows at his back and waited for Mum to continue.

"Just imagine for a minute, Seb, that everyone only does what is expected of them. They have no choice; rather they are just programmed to do certain things. Do you think God would get any pleasure from this type of mechanical obedience? Do you get any pleasure when you turn on the tap and the water always comes out?"

Seb gave Mum a puzzled look. "That's what it's supposed to do."

"Exactly. The tap doesn't see you across the room and say, 'Oh, there's Seb! I know he likes water to drink sometimes, or maybe to wash his hands. To please him, I'll release a flow of water.' Instead, it comes out because you turned the tap on and that's what it was manufactured to do."

Seb smiled at Mum's analogy. It was pretty ridiculous to think of such a scenario. "So I guess that when you take away the will to do evil, you take away the will to do good."

Mum nodded. "That's it, Seb. The words 'evil' and 'good' aren't relevant if there is no free will."

Seb thought about Mum's words. He could see what she meant, that one was a contrast of the other.

“But the main reason for free will is love. If we are like machines, programmed to do this or that, we won’t have the capacity to choose whether to love someone or not.”

“Because love is a choice,” Seb murmured.

“Exactly,” agreed Mum. “Some people think that love is involuntary, a feeling that comes over us, which we can neither conjure up nor resist, but really, it’s much, much more than that.”

“So if we’ve no free will, we can’t choose to obey or disobey, and neither can we choose to love. And love doesn’t even make sense if the choice to love doesn’t exist.”

Mum smiled. “Isn’t it remarkable that God, the Creator of the entire universe, so desired our love and obedience that He decided that it was worth the price of creating us with a free will?”

Seb nodded. “I guess it’s not only our love to God, but our love for fellow humans too. If we hadn’t the capacity to love God, we wouldn’t be able to love anyone.”

“You’re right. We can treat each other in one of two ways – we can hurt them and try to harm them, or we can love them and care for them.”

“So while free will gives us the option of mistreating people, it also gives us the option of loving them.” Seb grinned. It now made so much more sense. People who said that God could have made people without the capacity for evil really hadn’t thought it through. He figured no one would want to be like a robot with no control over their actions.

"Now, all this discussion has made me thirsty." Mum stood up and brushed a wisp of dark blonde hair from her face. "I'm going to make some tea. Want some?"

Seb swung his legs off the bed. "I'd love one of those snowballs you made and a mug of milk."

Mum smiled. "Thanks to Karen for the recipe. We used to love making them when we were little girls, but I couldn't remember the quantities of the ingredients. I'm glad she kept all of our mum's recipe books."

Seb followed Mum through to the kitchen and pulled out two of the new beige mugs, then lifted the milk from the fridge. All the talk of free will had brought the topic of his visit to Dad into his mind. Choosing to visit Dad and show him love was certainly a product of free will. He hadn't managed to tell Mum yet. He'd either been at the farm or she had been working, so this was the first opportunity they'd really had to talk.

Mum stirred the teabag around in the hot water, then dumped it in the bin. Seb grabbed the tin of coconut-covered biscuit and marshmallow treats. They pulled out chairs and sat at the table.

"Mum–"

"Seb–"

They both spoke at once.

Mum laughed. "You go first." She sipped her tea and reached for a snowball.

"Okay," Seb agreed. He was almost scared he'd chicken out if he didn't speak now. "I've decided to go and visit Dad."

Mum gave a slight smile. "Of your own free will, Seb?"

"Of course. I need to go and tell him that God loves him." He bit his lip. He'd felt a lot more courageous last week; now he was beginning to have second thoughts. "I'm not sure how he'll take it though. You know what he's like when someone mentions the Bible or God or Christianity to him."

Mum gave a dry laugh. "Oh, I know all about it, Seb."

"Mum…" Seb hesitated.

"What is it?"

"Why is Dad like that? I mean, he gets really angry and vicious. Like, unreasonably angry. It doesn't make sense to me."

"I'm not entirely sure, Seb. He always refused to talk about it, but I do believe there is a reason. Gran hinted at something in their past which seemed to affect your dad greatly as he was growing up, but I don't know any details."

It was extremely unlikely that Dad would want to open up to Seb, but he couldn't help wondering what it was that had turned Dad so completely against God.

"Anyway, Seb, if you're sure, I'll phone tomorrow and organise the date and time. Remind me to send written permission for you to go and visit him on your own."

Seb's stomach flipflopped and he set down his second snowball. Was he sure? No, not really, but he knew that this was what God wanted him to do. And really, his dad was in prison. There would probably be a prison officer present, someone to restrain him if he began to get violent. "That's fine."

Mum smiled. "You're a good son, Seb. Your dad might not realise it, but he's very blessed to have a son like you, one who prays for him and loves him enough to visit him."

Did Seb love his dad? If love was a choice, then yes, he supposed he did.

"So, I think it's my turn now?" Mum's voice broke into his musings.

"Oh! Yes, I forgot you had something to tell me." Seb began to wonder what news Mum had. He hoped it wasn't something negative, something –

"I'm getting baptised!" Her face broke into a big smile.

Baptised. Mum. Seb hadn't even considered that she might be thinking about baptism.

"That's great." He tried for an enthusiastic tone.

"I'd always heard that believers should be baptised, but lately I've been coming across it frequently in my daily reading. I want to obey the Lord in my life, and this is one way I can do this."

"So when is the… ceremony?"

Mum laughed. "It's called the baptism. It will be in a couple of weeks' time. You'll be there, won't you?"

"Of course. I wouldn't miss it."

"I thought Mrs Thompson would like to come, and I'm going to ask some of my work colleagues as well. It's a public declaration of my faith in Christ, you know. And maybe some women I met in the shelter in Belfast, and..."

As Mum ran through a list of people she wanted to invite, Seb's mind drifted off. Deep inside, he wished that he was the one getting baptised. He'd been saved before Mum, after all. But his own thoughts of baptism had been pushed aside lately, with schoolwork, the farm and everything else that occupied his time these days. Once everything got back to normal, he'd find out how to go about getting baptised.

Chapter Twenty

"I think this must be it." Aunt Karen flipped on the indicator and turned in at the gate. An understated sign which read 'Visitors' Centre' was attached to the high chain-link fence surrounding the carpark. Seb wiped damp palms on his jeans. Why had he ever agreed to do this?

Aunt Karen smiled as she reversed into a space near the drab pebble-dashed building. "You'll be fine," she said. "God is with you."

Seb knew that, but thinking about his dad always produced the same unwelcome reaction – a combination of dread, guilt, fear and worthlessness. At least the nightmares had stopped. He hoped they wouldn't restart when he saw him again.

They made their way from the car to the building. "Your mum said that you get a bus from here to the prison." Aunt Karen held up a paperback book. "I'm going to catch up on some reading and get a coffee."

A group of people were milling around the visitors' centre, obviously there for the same purpose as Seb. An older lady, with a dark red coat, short grey hair and glasses, had taken a seat near the door, her walking aid beside her. A young man, with baggy tracksuit bottoms and an earring, leaned against the wall, one hand in his pocket, and the other holding a phone. A couple of well-dressed people waited patiently, standing straight with briefcases in hand, professionally detached from the surroundings.

Aunt Karen joined the queue for coffee and Seb hovered uncertainly near the door. Now that he was here, he didn't want to miss the bus. Not that he was looking forward to this visit. His stomach roiled and he crossed his arms over his midsection.

The young man looked up from his phone. "First visit?" he asked.

Seb nodded. He didn't realise that his apprehension was so obvious.

"You'll be fine. Do what you're told and it's a doddle. I've been loads of times." He laughed. "On both sides. It's better being on this side of a visit, believe me."

Seb gave a weak smile.

A minibus pulled up outside and the small crowd shifted towards the door. Seb looked back at Aunt Karen. She held her hands up together in a prayer pose and mouthed, 'I'm praying.'

Seb shot her a grateful look and turned to follow the old lady as she manoeuvred her walking aid through the door and slowly boarded the bus.

The journey was short. Too short. Seb had hardly time to compose himself before the tall, dull brown walls, topped with huge coils of barbed wire, came into view. Large metal gates met them as they drove up. The whole place was stark, oppressive and foreboding.

Seb swallowed. Despite being as nervous as a hen entering a foxhole, he was exceedingly glad that he was entering the prison as a visitor and not as an inmate. To be driven up to these gates, knowing that this would be your home for the next few weeks, months or years, must be awful beyond words. Seb felt a spark of compassion for Dad.

The check-in process was slow. Seb handed over Mum's written consent and his provisional driver's licence, glad that Uncle Matt had encouraged him to apply for it when he became the age to drive a tractor on the roads.

"We need to photograph you and scan your index finger," the officer said unsmilingly, then directed him through the process, instructing him where to stand, where to look, how to place his finger on the scanner and wait until it beeped.

"We'll be keeping the photo and finger scan on record, so you won't need to bring ID next time."

Next time! If Seb could only manage to get through this visit.

Seb handed his phone and wallet to the prison officer who was storing belongings. "You can keep a few coins with you, but do you have anything else?" the official asked.

Seb shook his head.

The official gestured for Seb to move on and he made his way to the officer wearing blue gloves who was waving him forwards. Seb stood as instructed, feet apart, as the officer gave him a full rub-down search. He'd known this was part of the rules, but wasn't prepared for the close proximity of the officer, or the way he made sure that Seb wasn't smuggling even the smallest item into the prison. As he felt around Seb's shoulders, his head inches away from Seb's, a sudden memory flitted through his mind. "You're in my *personal space,*" one of the girls at his last school had always shrieked if someone got too close. He swallowed down the nerve-induced giggle before the officer noticed. The atmosphere in the place was hard and cold, and Seb knew instinctively that jokes in such a setting would be highly inappropriate.

Seb was directed forwards with another wave of the officer's hand, this time to walk past a large German Shepherd. Seb knew that the dog was here to detect drugs, but this one was nothing like the small, bouncy Springer Spaniel who had accompanied the police officers on their search of Dad's house. The dog leaned forwards and the large black muzzle sniffed Seb, then, seemingly satisfied, let him walk past.

Doors clanked open and shut, and Seb found himself in a large room with tables and chairs. As he followed the officer to a table, he could see the older lady struggle to her feet to greet a scrawny middle-aged man with a comb-over and droopy moustache. Probably her husband, Seb thought, but then quickly realised that the man was more likely to be her son.

"Wait there." The officer spoke to Seb, and he turned his attention away from the older lady. He took a seat where the man indicated, and waited.

Seb was watching the door, but still started when it noisily opened. A prison officer entered, followed by a large man dressed in a sweatshirt and jogging bottoms. Dad. Seb's heart leaped to his throat. He was going to be sick. He swallowed once, twice. Tried to slow his breathing. Closed his eyes.

When he opened them again, Dad was being led across the room. His eyes flicked towards Seb and away again and his face was expressionless except for the permanent sneer. He'd worn it so long that it had become embedded into the lines of his face.

He dropped into the seat and regarded Seb with a look of disdain. "So, the dutiful son has agreed to come and visit his delinquent father in jail, huh?"

Seb took a breath. Prison hadn't improved Dad's attitude towards him.

"Well, aren't you going to speak?"

Seb cleared his throat. He felt as tongue-tied and helpless as he always did around his dad. The noise of the other visits going on around him made it difficult to think what he should say. He glanced at the vending machines. "Do you want a tea or coffee?" he blurted out.

Dad frowned. "I'd like something stronger than that," he muttered. "But, if you're offering, I'll take a tea. Some chocolate too."

Seb pushed back from his seat and headed across the room. He didn't think he could eat anything, and if he tried to drink tea, he would probably spill it over himself, he was shaking so much. But he needed to step away, to try to regroup, before carrying on a conversation.

He carried the food back to the table and pushed Dad's tea and chocolate bar towards him. Lifting his carton of juice, he pulled the straw off the side and poked it into the small foil circle. It took a few tries before it pierced through.

"So your mother sent you." Dad set down his tea as if it had tasted like poison. "Cowardly woman."

Seb felt anger rising inside him. For Mum to always do everything Dad told her would have been cowardly. Instead, she'd had the courage to leave an abusive relationship.

"She didn't send me. She told me you wanted to see one of us, and it was my decision." Was he being less than honest if he didn't tell Dad that he had refused to come at first?

"So why did you decide to come? To tell me all about the cosy wee life you and that mother of yours have settled into? Or to tell me that I'm a desperately wicked person who deserves all I've got?" Dad's voice was mocking.

"No. I-I wanted to come and see you, to tell you–" He glanced around the room, disconcerted when he met the firm, observant gaze of a prison officer.

"Maybe you want to tell me you're sorry for all the hassle you've caused me?" Dad interrupted. "Don't think I don't know that it was you who tattled on me."

Seb froze. How could Dad know that? Was that why he had

requested this visit? Or, perhaps, was he only guessing? Seb decided to assume the latter. He wouldn't answer that question. He took a deep breath. "I wanted to tell you that God loves you." There. It was out.

Dad's face turned red and he lifted a clenched, meaty fist. The prison officer rushed forwards, ready to restrain Dad.

Seb figured he might as well get it all out. After all, Dad would probably never request another visit from him again. He breathed out a quick prayer for help, then rushed out his words. "I know you don't believe it, but it's true. There is a God, and He loves you, despite what you've done, how you've sinned against Him. He gave His Son to die on a cross so that you might be forgiven, and you can be, if you trust Him for your soul's salvation."

Silence.

Seb looked up and braced himself. He was certain that Dad would be about to explode with rage.

Instead, Dad was staring at him, eyes wide, mouth open. Finally, he gave a dry chuckle. The prison officer halted somewhere near their table, then slowly shook his head and made his way back to the edge of the room.

A chuckle? Dad was laughing?

"Seb, you've more courage than sense, I'll give you that." He laughed again. "Persistent. Why do you keep harping on at me like this? You know I'm an atheist."

Seb swallowed. Here was his opportunity. He tuned out the other conversations, the unfamiliar surroundings, the eyes of the officers. "Dad, why are you an atheist? I've often wondered."

"Seb, why don't you believe in Santa Claus? Or the tooth fairy?" He let out a guffaw of laughter. "Or maybe you do!"

"No. I don't."

"Because they don't exist, right?"

Seb nodded.

"So why do I believe there's no God? Because He doesn't exist. I don't have to ask you to prove to me there's no tooth fairy. So why are you asking me to prove there's no God?" He took a sip of tea, then bit off a large chunk of the chocolate bar.

"I'm not. I'm asking you why you're choosing to ignore the evidence for God and refusing to believe He exists. Were you always an atheist?"

"Ever since that..." He trailed off and waved a hand in the air. "Why does it matter? As long as I saw sense."

So there was a story. Something, or someone, had triggered Dad's violent hatred of Christians and had caused him to turn away from the belief that God exists. Dad hadn't always been an atheist. Seb knew that many people became atheists due to the influence of some teachers and lecturers, or when they came across the theory of evolution in their education. He didn't know much about Dad's childhood, but he was pretty sure that he hadn't been an enthusiastic pupil at school, neither had he gone to university. Others rejected the idea of the existence of God when they couldn't handle the question of evil and suffering. He sighed when Lavinia's question flitted through his mind. He hoped she wasn't going to be one of these.

"You're deep in thought." Dad was looking at Seb strangely over the rim of the cardboard cup. He was obviously waiting for a comeback from his last argument. What was it? Something about it not mattering?

"It does matter. You may be rejecting an interpretation of what you think God's like and not what He really is."

Dad frowned. "Some think He's like a generous Santa Claus, others that He's angry and controlling, and others think they can make bargains with Him. Who's right? Who knows what God's like? And who cares? He doesn't exist. Full stop." He crumpled the chocolate bar wrapper and dropped it onto the table.

Seb paused. There was something about Dad's argument that didn't make sense.

"Can you ask your mother if she'll send me some clothes? And a wee bit of money?" Dad changed the subject.

"I'll say to her," Seb agreed.

"Good. They've given me clothes, but Julie knows what I like."

"What's it like in here?"

Dad shrugged. "It's prison. I'd rather not be here. I shouldn't be here."

Seb frowned. Surely Dad realised that importing Class A drugs was most definitely a criminal offence?

"So tell me what's happening out there. In the real world."

Seb bit the inside of his lip. What could he tell Dad that he'd be interested in? Nothing about the farm, that was for sure. Neither would Dad want to hear about Seb's Bible study. And he probably shouldn't tell him that he and Mum had moved to the country – what if Dad was released sooner than they expected and came to find them?

"Nothing much," he finally said.

"What about school? Still the class swot?" He laughed, a loud uproarious burst which rose above the other conversations in the room.

Seb tried not to wince. "Not really," he said.

They sat in silence for a few more minutes. Seb wondered if he should return to the subject of God's love. Maybe Dad had heard enough for one day, though.

"Time up!" the guard called.

Seb breathed a sigh of relief.

"You'll come again?"

Dad wanted him to come back? Seb found himself nodding. "Yes. I'll come back." He watched as the officer led Dad from the room. What a strange visit! Apart from the initial flaring of his temper, he'd been relatively calm, and had acted almost... *normal*. Seb could only pray that what he'd been able to say had given his dad something to think about during his quiet hours alone.

He pushed up from the seat and made his way through the various sets of doors, signing out and collecting his belongings. During the process, Dad's words ran through his head. *Some think He's like a generous Santa Claus… Who knows what God's like? He doesn't exist.* Something didn't add up. As he ruminated over the words, suddenly it flashed into his mind. How could someone have a personality, yet not exist? Dad was saying, in effect, God might be generous, or angry, or bargaining, but He isn't real. Did Dad really believe there was no God, or could it possibly be that, down deep, He knew that God was real, but had chosen to ignore that fact? Because if Dad acknowledged that there was a God, He would have to face up to the fact that one day he would meet Him, and all his sins would have to be dealt with.

Chapter Twenty-One

"It's happened again." Uncle Matt set down the phone and rubbed a hand over his face. Seb and Lavinia had walked through the back door after school and caught the tail end of the phone conversation with Derek. It had been immediately obvious something was wrong.

Lavinia stepped further into the office, dropping her school bag in the corner of the room. She brushed aside a pile of invoices and propped herself on the corner of the desk. "Antibiotics again?" she asked, eyes wide.

Uncle Matt nodded. "The last time I wondered if someone had genuinely forgotten to dump the milk. This time though…"

"Do you think someone is doing this on purpose?" Seb asked, leaning against the doorframe.

"That's what I'm wondering. As far as I can tell from a quick scan of the medicine records on the computer, there aren't even any cows in the milking herd that have been treated in the past couple of days or might still be in the withdrawal period at this stage. Am I right, Vinnie?"

Lavinia nodded.

Seb ingested this information. So the antibiotics had come from another source.

"But who would do this?" Lavinia stood up and paced around the room. "What possible motive could anyone have?"

"And how could they do it?" added Seb. "Especially since you're now the only one with the key to the medicine cupboard."

"Did anyone get the key?" Lavinia stopped pacing and resumed her position on the corner of the desk.

Uncle Matt shook his head. "No. I have it hidden away and no one has asked me for it."

"So someone must have brought antibiotics here."

Seb chewed his lip as he pondered. Old Tommy was a lifelong friend of Uncle Matt's and the very idea of him trying to cause problems for Matt was nothing short of preposterous. Who else had access to antibiotics? Seb certainly didn't, and since neither Dale nor Lavinia knew where Uncle Matt's key was, neither did they. That left Caleb. "Sort of cuts down the suspects," Seb said.

Lavinia narrowed her eyes at him. "You don't think that Tommy did it, do you?"

"Of course not. That's ridiculous."

She shook her head slowly. "I can't believe you still think Caleb is responsible."

"I didn't say he was!"

"You implied it. I don't like your insinuations."

Uncle Matt sighed. "Vinnie. Seb. Stop arguing. It's not very helpful right now."

Seb closed his eyes. Uncle Matt was right. Arguing would solve nothing. Instead, what they needed was evidence.

"What's going on?" Dale's voice came from the doorway. Seb stood aside to let him enter.

"Antibiotics in the milk again," Uncle Matt replied wearily.

Dale's eyes widened. "Oh, Matt. Not again."

"Can't be an accident, Dale. Not this time."

Dale's mouth was a flat line. "We need to find out who's doing it."

"It's not you, me or Vinnie, and Tommy would never do such a thing... " Seb said, glancing warily at his cousin as he spoke.

"So it has to be Caleb," Dale finished.

Lavinia glared at him.

"In fact, I saw Caleb this morning, heading back into the parlour after all the milking was done and I had washed everything down."

Uncle Matt frowned. "After the cows were gone? Do you think that the antibiotics were put straight into the tank rather than injected into the cows, Dale?"

Dale looked blank for an instant. "Why, yes!" he said. "If someone wanted to sabotage the milk, wouldn't that be an easier way to get the antibiotics into it?"

"It would certainly explain the high concentration of antibiotics one day and none at all the next," Matt muttered. "If a treated cow was the problem, the level should drop more gradually than that."

"What makes you think that Caleb was going back to sabotage

the milk?" Lavinia was glowering at Dale. "Maybe he'd forgotten something, like his phone."

Dale snorted. "Vinnie, you've nailed it. He *did* 'forget' his phone." Dale rolled his eyes and lifted his hands in the air to form quotation marks. "I saw it sitting when I was leaving. What young person nowadays leaves their phone down and only remembers about it forty-five minutes later?"

"You think he left it there on purpose?" Matt asked. He didn't look at all convinced.

"That's a possibility," Dale replied. "You have to admit that he has a motive."

"I can't see it," Matt replied. "I know he isn't happy with me right now, but this seems out of proportion. It's just not like him – he's usually very sensible."

Dale shrugged. "Young men aren't always rational, Matt." He gave a chuckle. "We had plenty of irrational moments when we were younger, too."

"We never did anything as serious as this."

"Mummy wants to know if you're coming for your tea." Martha's little voice broke into the conversation. "She says the muffins are nicer when they're still warm."

Seb ruffled his cousin's hair. "What kind of muffins, Martha?"

"Coconut and… " She pursed her lips in concentration. "Lime!" she finished triumphantly.

"Sounds good, princess," Matt smiled at his blonde-haired daughter. "Did you bake them?"

"I measured out the coconut."

"Then they'll be the very bestest, most coconuttiest coconut and lime muffins ever."

"Silly Daddy!" Martha giggled, as she skipped back to the kitchen ahead of the rest.

Matt reached down for his crutches, then levered himself out of the seat. "Best not to say anything about your suspicions in front of Martha, Dale. Little ears hear just as well as big ears, and Martha picks up everything."

Dale nodded in agreement, but Seb could tell that they hadn't heard the end of it. He didn't like to think that Caleb was to blame – he'd always liked the neighbours' son – but the evidence certainly seemed to be pointing in his direction.

"What I can't understand..." Lavinia leaned her arms on the bar of the gate and paused as the cow gave another bellow. Satisfied that the soon-to-be mother was doing okay, she continued, "Is why Dale would allow Caleb to leave without his phone. And why did he not take it to him when he was leaving the parlour himself?"

"I asked him about that," Seb replied. "He said that he figured that it wouldn't do Caleb any harm to be without his phone for a little while, but when he was leaving the parlour, Caleb was nowhere to be seen, so rather than trudge all over the farm with it, he knew he'd come back when he missed it." Seb thought it was a perfectly reasonable explanation.

"Which he did. And now Dale thinks he was responsible." She paused. "I mean, he doesn't even know Caleb. It's very unfair accusing someone he only met about a week ago."

"No one else has access to the parlour, Vinnie."

She frowned. "Well, there has to be someone else. It just isn't making–" Suddenly she swung around to face Seb, eyes wide. "Hey! There is someone else! I can't believe we didn't think of him before now."

Seb blinked.

"The tanker driver! Seb," she caught his arm and shook it, "it's Trevor! He's the one who's been doing this."

Trevor. The milk collection lorry driver. The one Uncle Matt reported for drunk driving. Someone who might want to get even with Matt, who would be holding a grudge. Why hadn't they thought of this before now?

"It makes perfect sense!" Lavinia's voice rose above the noise of the cow's bawl. "The milk's usually collected when we're off to school and Dale is finishing his breakfast. No one would see him."

"But was he the one who collected the milk this morning? And the last time this happened?"

"Oh. I don't know." Lavinia looked a bit crestfallen.

"We'll need to find that out before we make any rash assumptions." Seb glanced at the cow. Two cream-coloured hooves were beginning to protrude. "But for now..."

"A heifer, Dad," Lavinia called as they entered the living room. Seb plopped down on the floor and leaned against the coffee table. He watched Lavinia sprawl onto the armchair beside the fire and brush a piece of straw off her sleeve.

Uncle Matt smiled from his position stretched out on the sofa. "Great job, Vinnie. All okay?"

"Yep. As easy as pie. I wish they were all as straightforward."

Her dad smiled. "I'm thankful for blessings like this, Vinnie. God doesn't have to give us anything, but a safely-delivered heifer calf is a blessing I'm very thankful for, all the same."

"Pity He didn't stop Trevor from sabotaging the milk."

Matt frowned and lifted himself up on one elbow. "What did you say, Vinnie?"

"I said that it's a pity–"

"Did you say Trevor?" interrupted Dale from the rocking chair.

Both men stared at Lavinia, heads forward and dark eyebrows

lowered. Seb thought that they'd never looked more alike than at this moment.

"Yes! I don't know why we didn't think about him."

"Vinnie..." Seb broke in.

She glanced at him, then back at her dad. "Well, we need to find out if he was the one who collected the milk those days."

"Dale?" Matt looked at his cousin.

Dale shrugged. "I don't know, Matt. I was already inside for breakfast."

"I'm sure there's some way to find out. Tommy might have been here. Or maybe Caleb was still around." Lavinia glanced at Dale as she spoke.

He raised an eyebrow at her.

"I'll phone Derek in the morning," Matt said. He looked thoughtful. "We need to know for sure."

"Derek won't be too happy if he thinks you're suspecting one of his drivers of sabotaging our milk," Seb commented.

Uncle Matt shook his head. "Probably not. But if he didn't lift the milk that day, then we needn't suspect him. I'll be diplomatic." He grinned.

"Dad's good at being diplomatic." Lavinia scrunched up her nose. "I didn't inherit that quality, unfortunately."

Seb laughed and got a glare from his cousin.

"Just because it's true doesn't mean you have to agree," she said, eyes flashing.

"I never spoke!" He held both hands up. Aunt Karen stepped into the room and Seb rose to his feet. "I think you'd better drive me home, Aunt Karen, before I get into trouble with Vinnie."

She narrowed her eyes at him. "Too late," she snapped, but Seb could see a smile playing at the corners of her mouth. He was glad that she was in a better mood. Caleb might have disappointed her lately, but Seb knew he still held a special place in Lavinia's affections, so the possibility of someone else being the culprit, rather than Caleb, seemed to be a load off her mind.

Chapter Twenty-Two

"Trevor was the driver," Lavinia said, grinning triumphantly. She waved her phone at Seb and sat down opposite him, then nabbed one of his chips. "Dad just texted to say."

"Hey, those are mine! Get your own chips." Seb batted her hand away from his plate.

"Just one, Seb!"

"You don't know how to stop at just one chip," he grumbled.

Rebekah giggled and pushed her plate over. "Have some of mine, Vinnie. I'll never finish all these."

"You sure?"

"Yes. Go ahead."

"So Uncle Matt phoned Derek, I take it?"

Lavinia nodded, lifting a chip from Rebekah's plate and dipping it into the ketchup on Seb's.

Seb rolled his eyes, but ignored her. "So did he admit to dumping antibiotics in the tank?"

"Well, I don't think Dad told Derek about our suspicions." She frowned.

"But didn't Derek wonder why he was asking?" Rebekah picked up a chip and delicately nibbled one end of it.

"I'm sure he probably did. I wish he'd told him so they could investigate and get to the bottom of it." Lavinia reached for Seb's bottle of water.

"No, Vinnie! I told you – get your own lunch!"

She lowered her eyebrows at him. "When Dad phoned the insurance company this morning, they said that they weren't going to pay out this time. We need to prove that it was Trevor."

Seb set down his chip. The insurance company weren't paying out? This was going to cost Uncle Matt a fortune.

"But how can you do that?" asked Rebekah. "Isn't the milk usually collected when you're at school?"

Seb scratched the back of his neck. "You're right. Unless we take off school, or go in late, we can't stay around waiting for Trevor to arrive."

"I'm sure Dale could do it. Or maybe even Dad. He's getting so much more mobile and he's really fed up being inside so much."

"Good idea," Seb said. "But how do we know when it's going to happen again? And won't Trevor get suspicious if someone is always around when he's lifting the milk?"

Vinnie lifted another chip from Rebekah's plate and slowly chewed. "When was the last contamination, Seb?"

"It was after I came back to town to live with Mum. A Wednesday,

I believe, because I was there to help with the milking when Derek phoned."

"And this one was also a Wednesday. Two weeks apart?"

Seb took a drink from his water bottle and lifted a forkful of baked beans. Was it two weeks? He could hardly remember. The weeks were blurring into one another.

"You went back to live with your mum three weeks ago," Rebekah said.

"Thanks, Rebekah!" Lavinia smirked. "It's great that you're so good at remembering all the little details about Seb's life."

Rebekah looked down at her plate, her cheeks warming at Lavinia's words.

"So do we think that the sabotager will strike again in another fortnight?" Seb moved the conversation back on track before Lavinia could tease Rebekah further.

"Sabotager? Is that even a word?" Lavinia scrunched up her nose.

"Saboteur," said Rebekah, giggling.

"Okay, then. Saboteur." He smiled at Rebekah. "English was never my strong point."

Seb caught Lavinia rolling her eyes. Just because her friendship with Caleb had gone belly-up…

"Did you ask Caleb if he saw anything?" Rebekah asked.

Seb looked towards Lavinia. "Did you, Vinnie? I haven't seen him for ages." Seb hadn't mentioned Dale's accusations about Caleb being the culprit to Rebekah. He was trying to ignore the lurking seed of suspicion that Dale had planted.

"He said he's seen Trevor around a few times, but he can't remember exactly when. And when he was there, Caleb was busy and didn't pay much attention to what Trevor was doing."

Seb pondered the possibility of Trevor being responsible. He certainly had a motive, but – "Does Trevor have cattle?" he asked.

Vinnie dipped another chip in Seb's ketchup and popped it into her mouth. "He lives here in town, but his dad has a farm and he helps out."

"So he would have access to antibiotics too."

It was looking more and more likely that the driver was responsible, but how could they prove it?

"Um, you don't think that some of Barry's gang might have organised it?"

Lavinia and Seb both turned to look at Rebekah. The possibility of the cattle rustlers getting their own back for their smuggling ring being broken up by the young people during the summer was an idea that neither of them had even considered.

"But how would they manage to get into the parlour?"

Rebekah shrugged. "I'd say there are many opportunities for someone to sneak in. Maybe while Dale is on another part of the farm, or away somewhere. It wouldn't be hard for those people to do something like this."

"I guess it's a possibility," Lavinia agreed. "Not all the people who were involved were caught."

Seb nodded. He knew that the people they had discovered rustling the cattle were only representative of a wider ring of criminals who operated in the area.

"So how will we know who is responsible?" Trevor, the rustlers, Caleb – all had a potential motive, some more compelling than others, and different times when they could have contaminated the milk. Would they ever discover the culprit?

"A test!" Lavinia suddenly exclaimed. "I can't believe I didn't think of it before now!"

"What?" Seb frowned. "Sure the milk is tested by the dairy and by then it's too late."

"No! We could take a sample from the tank before Trevor arrives and then if the dairy's test comes back positive for antibiotics, we can get our sample tested."

"Vinnie," Seb said, smiling, "you've got brains after all!"

The bell rang to signal the end of lunchtime, and Lavinia lifted her bag and slid from the chair. "Of course! I'm sure it's Trevor, and even if Dad doesn't see anything, well, the test will prove it."

"I wonder if Trevor, if that's who it is, will choose a Wednesday again?" Rebekah flicked a strand of blonde hair over her shoulder as she stood up.

"If that's the case, then we should concentrate on Wednesdays."

Seb joined the girls as they walked towards the door.

"Well, the milk is collected every two days, so the next time Trevor will be back on a Wednesday will be just under a fortnight."

"We'll have to remember to take a sample that morning," Lavinia said as she pointed right. "I need to run to my locker before class. See you in a minute."

She dashed off down the corridor. "She's cutting it fine today," laughed Rebekah. "And eating my lunch instead of buying her own? What was all that about?"

Seb shrugged. "I don't know. She probably just couldn't be bothered!"

"At least she chose to spend her lunchtime with us today for a change."

Seb agreed. Lavinia had hardly spent any time with them at school lately, but he figured that her new friend Jasmine didn't have the first clue about cows or bulk tanks, never mind sabotage by antibiotics.

"Come on, Seb! Finish up that tea. There are loads of beautiful ladies out there waiting for us."

Seb raised an eyebrow at Dale as he swallowed down the last of the tea and set his mug back on the table. Dale was entirely too chirpy for the beginning of Friday's evening milking.

By the time he rose from the table, Dale had already shoved his feet into his boots and had headed out the door. Seb put on his own boots and coat and followed him.

Throughout milking, Dale alternately whistled and burst into song, covering old classics, country songs, hymns and modern pop songs. Seb almost thought he saw the cows' ears twitching at the unusual noises in the parlour. No wonder. One minute, Dale finished off 'I'm gonna love you forever and ever, forever and ever,' with a deep, growly 'amen', then immediately followed with 'I'm dreaming of a white Christmas'.

What on earth was going on?

"Happy about something?" Seb asked mildly.

"Huh?" Dale broke off mid-chorus, still rocking his head slowly to the beat, a faraway look in his eyes.

"Are you happy about something?"

"Seb!" He laughed loudly. "I'm going *out* tonight! The first night in ages."

Goodness. If 'going out' makes Dale that happy, he must lead a pretty miserable existence, Seb thought as he lifted the clusters from the cow nearest to him.

Dale continued to whistle, hum and sing his way through milking. By the time milking was over, Seb's head was spinning. He was glad to get out to do the feeding to catch some peace and quiet.

When Seb made his way back to the house, Dale had already

showered and changed.

"All ready to go, Dale?" asked Matt from his usual position on the sofa.

"Yep, I'm ready." He lifted his jacket and slung it on, then patted his jeans pockets. "Got my phone, wallet and keys. I'll see you later." He laughed. "Or maybe not. Don't wait up." He pulled the door closed with a bang as he left, the odour of aftershave lingering in the air.

"Well, now. What's come over Dale tonight?" asked Aunt Karen in the sudden silence.

Matt chuckled. "He's on cloud nine, all right. My guess? He's found a girl."

"Aw, Dad! Really?" Lavinia's eyes were wide. "What makes you think that?"

"You didn't have to do the milking with him, Vinnie." Seb rolled his eyes. He burst into an impression of Dale's singing. Everyone howled with laughter when he lowered his chin and eyebrows for the 'amen'.

"But where on earth has he met her? I mean, this is the first night he's been out, isn't it?"

"Apart from that school reunion," Aunt Karen reminded them, pulling a casserole from the Aga.

"Nope." Lavinia shook her head. "He told me that most of the girls he went to school with are now married, and the ones who were at the reunion who are still single haven't aged very well. He said that some of them looked like beanbags in minidresses."

"Oh, Lavinia!" Aunt Karen shook her head while Uncle Matt sniggered.

"Those were his words, Mum, not mine. So unless he's found a girl in the supermarket or when he's been running messages for the farm, I don't know where he'd have met her."

"Well, there's no point in speculating." Aunt Karen divided the casserole onto plates and they all took their seats around the table. "We'll find out soon enough, I'd say."

Chapter Twenty-Three

"... I baptise you in the name of the Father, and of the Son, and of the Holy Spirit."

Seb watched as Mum was gently put under the water and brought back up. Water ran down her face. She tried to wipe it away, blinking rapidly, then reached for the towel that Aunt Karen was holding out to her.

"Up from the grave He arose, with a mighty triumph o'er His foes," the congregation sang heartily, as Mum made her way out of the baptismal tank.

"He arose a victor from the dark domain, and He lives forever with His saints to reign... "

Seb could see the look on Mum's face as she disappeared through the door at the front, Aunt Karen following behind her.

It was a look she had worn often since she'd trusted Christ, but never was it more pronounced, more joyous, than tonight.

"He arose! He arose! Hallelujah, Christ arose!"

It was a look of absolute peace and serenity.

"She did *what*?" Dad stared across the table at Seb, eyes wide. The conversations around the room blended into a chowder, fragments of sentences rising, then being replaced by others before they could be identified and understood.

"Got baptised," Seb repeated.

"I heard you the first time." Dad looked stunned. Almost as if someone had hit him over the head with something large and heavy and he hadn't yet fallen to the ground. "Why would she do that?" He shook his head and blinked.

"I guess she was being obedient to the Bible." Seb's own words pricked his conscience. He had the same Bible and there was nothing to prevent him from being baptised too. *Once Uncle Matt is well again*, he thought.

"Pah!" Dad spat, the stunned look being replaced by derision spreading across his face.

At least this was a reaction that Seb was familiar with. The one he'd expected initially from Dad.

"So she's serious about this Christianity business, then." His lip turned up in a sneer.

"Well, of course," Seb replied. "She's happier now than she's ever been."

"Now that I'm out of the picture, huh?" Dad narrowed his eyes at Seb.

Oh dear. This visit was not going well today. Seb took a deep breath.

"That's got nothing to do with it. It's because she's a Christian now. Her sins are all forgiven and she knows she's going to heaven."

"Nonsense, nonsense, nonsense." Dad leaned back in his chair and folded his arms. "It's all fairy stories. The whole lot of it."

"Did you always think like this?"

"Like what?"

"That the Bible is a collection of fairy stories?"

"Until I learned some sense." Dad laughed. "Seb, why don't you get me a cup of tea instead of getting geared up for a preach?"

Seb pushed his chair back and made his way to the vending machines. As he waited in the queue, he pondered. Why was Dad so reluctant to explain his reasons for his beliefs? And why had Seb never heard anything about Dad's childhood? He was becoming increasingly convinced that Dad's atheism was based upon something that had happened to him, rather than a study of scientific facts and morality.

He stuck a bottle of water under his arm and lifted the red and brown paper cup and two chocolate bars, and made his way back to where Dad was sitting. He was staring across the room, eyes unfocused, mind in another place.

Seb set the tea and chocolate in front of him and slid back into his seat. He unscrewed the top of the water bottle and gulped a quarter of the contents before setting it back down and opening the bar.

He was about to take a bite when he heard Dad speak.

"What was that?" Seb asked.

"He was cruel." Dad muttered. "Wicked man."

Seb blinked. "Who was?"

"He whipped me. With his belt. Left me with welts all down my legs. That wasn't the worst thing he did." Dad was still staring across the room, his eyes glazed over. "That time he poured the boiling water over my legs. So much pain." His eyes briefly closed, and when he reopened them he looked like a little lost boy, the hurt written on every inch of his face. "I needed surgery. And–" He choked up, then cleared his throat. "He told them that it had been an accident, that I had pulled the kettle down by mistake."

Seb's chocolate bar dropped from his hand, forgotten. He'd never guessed that Dad's father had hurt him so much. And what cruelty!

"He locked me in a cupboard. Told me there were poisonous spiders who would eat off my fingers and toes one by one if I made a noise." He gave a sound like a strangled chuckle. "Of course, he was lying, but I believed every word. I was there so long. Overnight. And so hungry." He rubbed his stomach. "I was hungry so much. For every small crime I was locked away and given no food. Then beaten."

"Did… did anyone know what was going on?" Seb asked softly. He was almost afraid to speak in case Dad suddenly realised that he had let down his guard, and clammed up.

"Mum knew. And my granny. No one else did, but no one could stop him anyway. He reigned in our family. No one questioned him. His word was law."

Seb toyed with the chocolate bar. Any appetite that he'd had was gone, swept away by sickness and revulsion that someone would treat a child with such cruelty. Dad's mistreatment of him had been more emotional, and Seb was thankful that he didn't have physical scars to match his emotional ones. Dad appeared to have both – long and deep, burned into his heart and soul.

"When did your dad stop hurting you?" Seb asked quietly. The noise and bustle in the background had faded until it felt as though only Seb and his dad were in the room.

Dad blinked and looked directly at Seb as if he'd only just realised he was there. "My dad?" he snorted. "He never hurt me. How could he, when he ran off before I was born?"

"You never knew your dad?" Seb was puzzled. "Then who… ?"

"My grandfather." Dad's lip turned up in a sneer again. "The forgiving and benevolent man who took his wayward daughter back when her no-good husband ran off and left her expecting a child." Sarcasm dripped like sticky honey from Dad's words.

"You grew up in your grandparents' house?" Why had Seb never known this before?

"The preacher and his wife." Dad snorted and shook his head. "What a hypocrite."

"He was a preacher?" Seb's eyes grew wide. Dad had grown up with his preacher grandfather, who physically abused him? No wonder Dad hated Christians!

"The holiest of the lot. His congregation adored him. Thought he was wonderful. He had the wool pulled over their eyes. Not one of them realised that their amazing preacher was a violent man at home, who beat his wife, daughter and grandson."

"Why did Gran stay?" Seb asked.

"She had me. She needed a babysitter and couldn't afford her own house."

Seb's mind was spinning with the irony of it all. Dad, the wife beater, the one who scorned and derided his only child, had actually grown up in a house where he had been a victim of abuse and hatred. He longed to ask Dad why he'd followed in the same path as his grandfather, with vicious outbursts of rage. At least now he could understand, in a measure, why Dad had no time for religion.

Dad looked directly at Seb. "Seb, when that man died, everyone kept talking about how much good he'd done, and how, because of that, he was surely in heaven. I made a vow. If that is the sort of people that God wants in heaven, then I want nothing to do with a God like that." He glanced off up to the ceiling. "He preached that God is love, yet I never saw one shred of love from that man. What he said about God was so far removed from the man, that I could only come to one conclusion." He leaned forwards and pierced Seb with a stare. "There is no God."

So now Seb knew. The reason for Dad's total hatred of Christians, God, the Bible. He had told him his story. To Dad, the very words that

Seb now loved so much raised feelings of hurt, bitterness and danger within his Dad's being. No wonder Dad had reacted so violently when Seb told him he was a Christian.

"Dad..." Seb began hesitantly. He bit his lip. How could he word this best?

"What is it?" Dad looked old and drained. Telling his story seemed to have raised memories that he had kept stuffed inside for years.

"You do know that not all Christians are hypocrites?"

Dad gave a slight smile. "So they say. I don't trust them."

"I can understand that. But there's more. Not everyone who claims to be a Christian really is one."

"Sure that's all there is to being a Christian! Just say you are one, and that's what you are. Who am I to argue with them?"

Seb immediately shook his head. "No, Dad. That's where you're wrong. A Christian is someone who has realised that they are only a sinner who deserves nothing but hell forever, but who trusts in the Lord Jesus Christ. He is God's Son, and He took their punishment so that they could go free and be in heaven forever."

"And so they can go back to living how they like."

Again Seb vigorously shook his head. "Absolutely not! When someone gets saved, they are changed forever. The Bible says they are a new creation. They have a personal relationship with God and so they want to live for Him, to please Him and do what He says."

"Like getting baptised?" Dad smiled wryly.

"Well, yes." Seb really would have to ask to be baptised very soon. "All I'm saying is that it really doesn't sound like your grandfather was saved. You said his congregation said that he was a good man, so he'd be in heaven. The Bible says that those who are in heaven aren't there by their own works but because of God's grace. Depending on good works will never get us there."

Dad grunted. "Well, I never saw too many good works anyway, and he certainly never talked about this 'saved' business that you seem so fond of mentioning."

"He probably wasn't truly a Christian." Seb felt a moment of sadness at the thought that his great-grandfather, a preacher, one who purported to know the truth, didn't actually know Christ at all. "And another thing," he went on, suddenly remembering something else he wanted to say, "Christians aren't perfect yet. They won't be until they are in heaven. We try to live for God, but sometimes we fail. We're always going to let people down."

Dad raised his eyebrows.

"If you want to know what a person is like, you don't look at his employees, or friends, or family. That might give you an idea of some of the person's characteristics, but it's not a true representation. Instead, you look at the person himself."

"You're talking about God." Dad actually looked thoughtful.

"Yes. He's the one you need to learn about. And the best way to do that is through reading the Bible. The gospels contain the account of the Lord Jesus Christ on earth. He is God and totally sinless, so when we read about Him, we learn about God's character."

Seb glanced up. The prison officer was approaching their table. It was time for Seb to leave.

"Dad," Seb sent up a fleeting, silent prayer, "if I sent you a Bible, would you read it?" He held his breath while Dad pursed his lips, deep in thought. It was a momentous decision for this man, the one who had spent so much of his life hating every mention of God. For Dad to agree to accept and read a Bible would be a miracle beyond what Seb had even hoped for.

The officer was almost at their table.

"Not much else to do around here," said Dad.

"So can I send you one?" Seb held his breath. Was Dad really agreeing to read the Bible?

"I said yes, Seb. Are you stupid?" Dad was shaking his head, but the sneer was gone.

Seb's grin split his face from ear to ear.

He could hardly believe it, but it was true.

Miracles still happened!

Chapter Twenty-Four

"Come here!" Lavinia waved frantically at Seb.

Seb frowned. What was so terribly urgent that she needed to talk to him right now?

"Why couldn't you just have come over to the table to talk to me?" he asked as he approached her.

"Because I need to go to my locker and you're coming with me."

"Woah, Vinnie. Hold on. You got me to leave my lunch to go with you to your locker." He rolled his eyes.

"No!" She thumped his arm. "I've something to tell you, but Mrs Craig wanted to see me right now and I still have to go to my locker. If I don't tell you now, I'll probably not get telling you until home time."

"Which is only two hours away. I don't think it would kill you to wait."

"Okay, then. If you don't want to know, go back to your lunch." She sniffed and turned her shoulder away.

"Ugh, Vinnie! Don't be like that. You might as well tell me now I'm here."

They reached the lockers and she narrowed her eyes at him. "If you really want to know..."

Seb rolled his eyes. She was going to make him grovel before she'd tell him. "Yes, Vinnie. I do want to know."

She pulled her books from her locker, then slammed the door shut and turned to him. The sparkle was back in her eyes. "I found out who Dale was seeing the other night."

Seb waited.

"Aren't you going to ask me who it was?"

Seb sighed. Oh boy, was his cousin hard work today. "Okay. Who was it?"

"Kate!" Her eyes danced.

"Kate?" Seb tried to think. Who was Kate? The name was familiar.

"Oh, Seb!" Lavinia groaned. "The receptionist at the vet's."

"Ah! I remember now. The talkative girl that your Dad gets frustrated with."

"That's her." Lavinia giggled. "Can you imagine her and Dale together?"

"I've never seen her. But how did you find out?"

"Mum was meeting a friend for lunch today in that wee place she likes near the vet's and who walked in but Dale and Kate. She nearly had kittens!"

"What did Dale do? Was he not embarrassed to be found out?"

She snorted. "No. Apparently he puffed out his chest and gave Mum a cheesy grin as if to say 'Hey, Karen, look at the bird that I've managed to get!'"

Seb laughed. He could envisage Dale doing what Lavinia was describing. "So what is Kate like?"

"Apart from being talkative? Oh, you know, bleach blonde, lots of makeup... She kind of looks like Dolly Parton."

Seb laughed. "Sounds just like what Dale would go for all right!"

Lavinia glanced at her watch and groaned. "Oh no. I better run. I'm so late. Mrs C won't be happy." She dashed off, leaving Seb chuckling.

He set off back to the canteen. Dale getting a girlfriend. Who would have thought it? Maybe Kate would be the one who would persuade him to leave New Zealand and come back home for good.

The next day, Lavinia caught Seb's arm as they left English class. "Did you forget that it's two weeks tomorrow since the milk was sabotaged? If Trevor is working to a schedule, then tomorrow will be the day."

Seb nodded. "I've been thinking about that. But surely he wouldn't be so stupid as to space out his sabotaging so evenly."

Lavinia raised her eyebrows. "I don't want to be stereotypical, but he's one of those guys who swallow steroids and are all muscle and no brain."

"I haven't met him yet, so I can't comment."

"It's a pity we don't get off school for Christmas until Friday. We really need to be at home tomorrow morning."

"But your mum won't let you take the day off."

"Not unless I'm sick. Like, half-dead sort of sick." She rolled her eyes.

Seb laughed. They were almost at the geography classroom door. "Honestly, Vinnie, I think your best option is to take a sample of the milk before Trevor arrives. And for conclusive proof, get your Dad to hang around the parlour. I mean, now that he has the cast off, he's really getting much more mobile, isn't he?"

"Oh yes. Hopefully he'll be able to ditch the crutches soon, although they say his leg will never be quite the same again."

Seb still felt awful that the accident had ever happened, but it could have been much worse.

"I'll speak to him, then. It'd be better if we caught Trevor in the act. Maybe Dad could hide in the parlour or something. If he talks to him, then he won't do it and we need to prove that it was him, so we can at least get the money back that Dad had to pay the dairy."

"Just make sure he videos it on his phone, if he can," Seb said, entering the classroom and heading for a free seat beside Danny. He watched as his cousin scanned the room, then made her way to where Jasmine was sitting.

“So how did your dad get on? And did you get a sample this morning?” Seb asked as they stepped off the bus together on Wednesday afternoon. It was almost dark, the product of an overcast day coupled with the approaching winter solstice.

Lavinia gave her head a little shake. “I was running late and I left it with either Dale or Dad to take it. I didn’t actually hear from Dad all day. I texted him earlier, but he didn’t reply.”

They crossed the road and made their way up the lane. “I wonder why he didn’t let you know. Do you think it’s because nothing happened, or he caught him and has been tied up all day with police and legal stuff?”

“I don’t know. I hope the latter, but I have a feeling that it was probably your first suggestion.”

They rounded the corner of the yard and entered the house. As usual, Lavinia threw open the office door and was about to launch her schoolbag into the room when she spotted her dad on the phone. Seb could see him turning and frowning, then waving them out of the room. Lavinia closed the door softly and went into the kitchen instead.

“Who’s Dad on the phone with?”

Aunt Karen was cutting slices of a pale loaf with a sugary topping and arranging them on a plate.

“I’m not sure,” she said. “He’s been in there most of today, going through invoices and bills.”

Lavinia shrugged out of her blazer and washed her hands, while

Seb plopped himself down at the kitchen table.

"He didn't say anything about Trevor?" Lavinia asked.

"Trevor? No, he didn't mention him at all today."

The door opened and Matt made his way into the kitchen. He looked exhausted, dark circles under his eyes.

"Dad, did you catch Trevor earlier?"

Matt gave a wry smile. "Good to see you too, Vinnie. My day was great, thanks for asking."

"Sorry, Dad! Hello. How was your day?"

Matt gave a low chuckle. "Give me a minute to sit down and then I'll tell you the latest."

Lavinia pulled out her dad's seat and waited until he sat down, then – "Well?"

"Karen, this one takes after you!" Matt shook his head. "Impatient as a bee before a big storm."

"Dad…" Lavinia was beginning to sound exasperated.

"Okay, okay! No, I did not catch Trevor earlier. I managed to clatter my crutch against the door. He obviously heard me so I had to walk through as if I'd just been inspecting the parlour."

"Well, did you get a sample before he arrived?"

"I'm afraid not, Vinnie. There was a little breakdown in communication between me and Dale."

Lavinia groaned. "Oh, Dad!

"Trevor was just about to attach the hose to the tank, so I don't believe he was going to do anything anyway."

"Ah well. I take it that the milk was okay today, then."

Matt sighed. "Actually, Vinnie, that's where you're wrong. There *were* antibiotics in the milk. Derek phoned earlier, and that phone call you barged in on? That was the insurance company. They definitely won't pay out this time. I thought it wouldn't hurt to ask."

Seb sat frozen with shock. Again?! For the third time? Someone, somewhere had a huge grudge against Uncle Matt. What possible motive could they have?

"Dad!" Lavinia quavered. "How is that even possible? Trevor *must* have done it. Do you think he put the antibiotics directly into the sample and not the tank after all?"

Matt shrugged. "Vinnie, I don't know. We do need to get to the bottom of this. To be perfectly blunt…" He looked around the room. "Where's Martha, Karen?"

"She's upstairs, playing with her dolls."

Satisfied that his younger daughter wasn't within earshot, Matt continued, "This sabotage is leaving us desperately in debt. With the knock we've had from the TB test and the resulting loss of income, as well as paying labourers that I wouldn't normally have to pay, we're going to be seriously struggling in the new year. One more milk sabotage might be enough to put us under."

Lavinia looked horrified. "You mean we'd have to, like, sell the farm?"

Matt nodded slowly. "Or at least some of it."

Seb's heart dropped to his boots. He felt the room tilt and he grabbed the table. Surely not. He couldn't imagine life without Cherryhill Farm. What about the cows? What would the McRoss family do? Uncle Matt was a farmer. He'd invested much of his life into making the farm work and support his family.

Seb felt sick. Whatever happened, they couldn't let Cherryhill Farm be lost.

The milk saboteur needed to be stopped. And fast.

Chapter Twenty-Five

After milking, Seb found Lavinia huddled with Glen and Jess halfway up the pile of straw bales. "Vinnie," Seb called as he began to climb the bales to join her.

She lifted her head and Seb could see the evidence of tears on her face. He sat down beside her, and Glen moved over to curl up on his knee. "Glen, pup, you're getting a bit big for this," he said, but wrapped his arms around the wriggly dog anyway. Seb turned to his cousin. "How are you doing?" he asked.

Lavinia sniffed and her lip wobbled. "I can't believe how awful things are right now. It seems that nothing is going right."

"At least we haven't had too much trouble with calving."

"If you don't count the dead heifer calf when Dad was in hospital."

"That was tough, but there have been so many other living ones."

"Not much use if we have to sell them all." She pulled a ragged tissue from her pocket and blew her nose loudly.

They were silent for a few moments, then Lavinia spoke again. "How could God let this happen? I mean, what has Dad done to deserve it? He always puts God first."

Seb nodded. What she'd said was true. And yet, that was no guarantee of a storm-free life. "What about Job? You know the story. Job was a good man, yet he lost his children, his animals and his health. The Bible says that even though he lost almost everything, he didn't sin or say anything against God. I believe Job learned lessons from his experience, and so did his friends who insisted he must have done something wrong to deserve all his trials."

"So you think God's trying to teach someone something by taking away the farm? Nice." Her mouth settled in a hard line.

"Vinnie, I know it's hard, but we don't know what's best for us."

"And God does?" She turned to him, hurt and anger sparking in her brown eyes.

"Of course!" Seb was startled by her outburst. "God's wisdom far exceeds ours." He paused, contemplating the distance between man's supposed wisdom and God's omnipotence. "This isn't really an accurate picture," he said at last, "but it's kind of like when Martha wants to do something that your parents know is dangerous."

"Like riding her bike to Tommy and Madge's?" asked Lavinia, quirking an eyebrow.

Seb smiled. His little cousin had seen no problem with taking off down a busy road on her little pink bike, and hadn't been at all pleased when Aunt Karen had stopped her and confiscated her bike. "Yes, like that. Martha couldn't see the danger, she didn't know that she could have been killed. Your mum has greater knowledge and more wisdom than Martha has, and even though it hurt Martha to be told no, it was ultimately for her greater good."

Lavinia pursed her lips and narrowed her eyes. "I guess I see where you're coming from, but I don't think that removing the farm is very kind."

"No one said the farm was being removed," Seb reminded his cousin. "God might allow the farm to be sold, but He would have a purpose in that and His plans are always for our ultimate good. But, on the other hand, it might not be His will, and He's maybe going to work a miracle and step in to save the farm so that He will be glorified."

Lavinia sighed. "Well, let's hope it's the latter. And let's hope that He saves it very soon."

Seb was glad that, for now, his cousin seemed to be accepting the reality of God's existence. He figured that deep down she'd never really stopped believing that God existed, and he prayed that, instead of causing her to question things, these trials would make her realise that she needed Christ after all.

Lavinia stroked Jess's ears. "This isn't going to be a very good Christmas."

"One week until Christmas Day. Not how I thought my first Christmas away from Belfast would turn out either. Maybe next year we'll have a better Christmas."

"If we're still at Cherryhill," Lavinia said.

The door to the shed creaked open and Dale stepped in. "Oh, there you two are. I didn't know where you were."

Jess's ears pricked up at the sound of Dale's voice and Glen gave a low rumble in his throat.

"Just keep those monsters up there," Dale said, laughing nervously. "I just wanted to tell you that another cow has just calved. A bull calf this time, but all went well."

Lavinia gave a slight smile. "That's great, Dale. Thanks."

He lifted a hand and waved as he left the shed.

"I don't know what these two have against him," Seb stroked the hackles back down on Glen's back.

Lavinia shrugged. "I think they can detect the fear and it brings out their hunting instinct." She rubbed her arms. "I'm getting cold. I think I'll go inside now."

She stood up and made her way down the bales, Jess climbing down beside her. Seb dumped Glen off his lap and the puppy bounded down, losing his balance and rolling to the bottom. Seb laughed as he watched him pick himself up, give himself a good shake, then run off after his mother.

"Do you think we'll have snow for Christmas?" he asked as they walked back to the house.

"It's cold enough for snow, but Christmas is still a week away."

"A white Christmas would be good." Seb laughed. "At least that's what Dale was dreaming about in the milking parlour the other night."

"What did he say about there being antibiotics in the milk again?"

she asked.

Seb paused. Again, he'd been insistent that he'd seen Caleb at the tank, but he didn't want to tell Lavinia and make her angry again. "He seemed surprised. I didn't tell him what your dad said about the farm being in trouble. I didn't think that was something that he should hear from me."

"I'm sure he doesn't need to be told. He knows how much we need to pay the dairy each time it happens. He's not stupid."

They reached the door and Lavinia pushed it open and headed inside. Seb looked up at the starry sky. He couldn't help but be reminded of the greatness of God, but despite his words to his cousin, he still felt dread at the thought of what could be ahead for this family and their farm. They needed to get to the bottom of the milk sabotage, and if it wasn't Trevor, then who was it? The rustlers? Or could it be Caleb? He knew Uncle Matt had talked to him, but Seb needed to resolve this for himself.

Tomorrow, he'd phone Caleb.

"It's snowing!" Rebekah lifted her face to the sky as big fluffy flakes drifted down onto her upturned face and blonde hair. "Just in time for Christmas!"

"Huh. It'll probably not last until then." Lavinia hoisted her bag onto her shoulder. "Come on, Seb. We don't want to keep Mum waiting. She's got lots to do."

Seb sent an apologetic smile Rebekah's way, then hurried after his cousin. The buses didn't run when there was a half day at school, so Aunt Karen had arranged to collect them. Seb was glad the term was over. He'd managed to keep up with the work, but barely, and he really didn't know how the exams were going to go in the new year. He'd worry about that problem some other time. There were plenty of things to think about before then.

"So how was school?" Aunt Karen asked as they climbed into the car.

"Pointless," replied Lavinia. "I told you they don't do anything on the last day. We'd have been better off helping out at home."

Aunt Karen started the car and joined the queue leaving the car park. "That may be so, but I'm not sure you're really too popular with your teachers this term."

"It's not my fault I'm behind on my work."

"I know that. The farm would never have managed without you both. Come the new year, things will hopefully get back to normal."

"Or they'll never be normal again," Lavinia muttered under her breath.

As they drove farther from town, the snow fell heavier and heavier, and by the time they reached the farm, the roads were white. "It certainly looks very Christmassy," Aunt Karen commented as she made the turn into the lane. The wheels spun a little as they climbed the lane, but they made it safely to the yard.

Inside, Martha was playing with her dolls in front of the fire.

"Late night again last night," Lavinia sniggered, pointing to Dale asleep in the armchair.

"Where's Matt, I wonder?" asked Karen.

"He went outside to check on a cow," said Martha as she tugged a vibrant pink dress over the head of a blonde doll and tried to poke the arms through the sleeves.

Aunt Karen frowned. "Seb, would you please pop out and check he's okay? I hope he isn't doing anything silly like trying to calve the cow."

Seb dumped his schoolbag and put on his wellies. The snow was falling faster now, the sky darkening with the heavy snow clouds. The flakes were swirling in front of him and he squinted against the dizzying effect. He was almost at the shed door when he saw something lying on the ground. A dark mound, sprinkled with snow. He peered through the snow as he came closer and his heart sank.

Uncle Matt.

He closed the distance and knelt down beside him. "Uncle Matt?" This was too familiar. Seb breathed a sigh of relief when his uncle spoke.

"Seb? Stupid crutches. I heard the car drive in and I tried to hurry back to the house, but then I slipped on a patch of snow and couldn't get back up. I think I've done something to my leg as well."

Seb looked around for the crutches, then shook the snow off them. "Can you get up at all?"

"If you give me a hand, I should be able to."

Between them, they managed to get Uncle Matt to his feet and then gingerly made their way to the house. Matt's face was pale.

"Matt! What have you done?" Aunt Karen met them at the door and helped him to the sofa.

"I just came down a rattle."

"You did that, all right! What about your leg?"

"Maybe you should phone that consultant guy. It feels a bit funny."

Aunt Karen closed her eyes. "Oh, Matt. I hope you haven't done any more damage to it." She lifted the phone and pulled a card from the letter rack. "I'm not sure if he'll be able to see you. He's maybe off for Christmas."

Half an hour later, Seb watched as Uncle Matt and Aunt Karen set off through the snow to the hospital. He prayed they'd make it there safely and that Uncle Matt's leg would be okay.

The afternoon dragged past. Lavinia served up the soup that Aunt Karen had prepared for lunch, then they took it in turns to stay inside with Martha while the others went outside to help with the work on the farm. When milking time came, Seb joined Dale in the parlour.

"This isn't what they needed right now," Dale commented. He still wore a happy grin despite the seriousness of the situation. Seb rolled his eyes. Love sure did weird things to people.

"Things have been tough for them lately," Seb said as he pulled off a length of blue roll.

"Yep. But Matt's always had it so good. Everyone hits bad times sooner or later."

Seb looked at Dale and frowned. If he didn't know better, he'd think that he was slightly pleased that Matt had hit this hard time. Couldn't be, though. They were cousins. Family. Dale was here to help in Matt's time of need. His tone of levity was only to do with a certain local blonde.

His thoughts turned to another local blonde, a younger and much prettier one. He hoped that they'd get to see the Harvey family over Christmas, although how Caleb and Lavinia would get on was anyone's guess.

Caleb.

Seb groaned. He'd completely forgotten to phone him yesterday. He really would have to chat to him soon.

Chapter Twenty-Six

"His leg will be okay, but he needs to rest it completely for a few days." Aunt Karen's voice coming through Lavinia's phone was faint, but Seb could still make out what she was saying. He breathed a sigh of relief. They'd all been worried that Matt had damaged his leg again, permanently this time. "We'll be home as soon as we can," Aunt Karen went on, "but the roads are really bad and I think Seb would be best staying the night."

Lavinia looked at Seb and pointed to her phone. "Can you hear her?" she mouthed.

Seb nodded. He'd already figured that he'd be staying overnight as he didn't know how soon Uncle Matt and Aunt Karen would get back from the hospital. He'd phoned Mum earlier, but maybe he should give her an update and let her know for sure that he wouldn't be home.

He lifted his phone and headed to the formal sitting room where it would be quieter and he wouldn't be disturbed. He turned on the light and flopped onto the sofa, then scrolled through his contacts. Caleb's name drew his attention. This would be a good time to chat to him, after he'd talked to Mum.

Mum wasn't at all surprised that he was staying overnight. She was fine, she was sipping hot chocolate and was curled up under a furry blanket with a book, she said, and there was no need to worry about her.

After he ended the call, he brought up Caleb's name, his finger hovering over the screen. What was he going to say? 'I don't believe that you are responsible, but I'm asking you anyway because I kind of do'? He thought for a minute, then shrugged. If he was going to make the call, he'd need to do it now, before he was gone for too long and someone came looking for him.

Caleb answered on the first ring. "Seb. How's things?"

"Doing fine, Caleb. Isn't that some amount of snow out there?"

They chatted about the snow, about Matt's fall and about Christmas. Seb knew he was stalling, trying to hold off on the inevitable conversation for as long as he could.

Finally there was a pause in the conversation. "Uh, Caleb…" Seb began.

"What is it?" Caleb sounded mildly worried.

"You know the milk sabotage that's been happening?"

"Yes?"

"I just wondered if you'd any ideas who might be responsible?"

"I thought Vinnie said that Trevor was the culprit."

Seb sighed. "We hoped that he was, but Uncle Matt didn't catch him the other day, although he dropped a crutch and kind of gave himself away."

"Trevor could have added the antibiotics to the sample. I don't know if the dairy checks the full load of milk when it arrives, or only the individual samples."

"That's a possibility." He swallowed. Might as well bite the bullet. "Uh, Dale says he saw you going back into the parlour when no one was around the mornings of those days."

Silence, then – "What's that got to do with it? I left my… Hey! Does Dale think I did it? That's absurd! I can't believe he'd suggest such a thing!"

Seb winced. Caleb had taken the accusation about as well as Seb had expected.

"Seb, please tell me you don't believe him. I mean, why would I even want to do such a thing to Matt and Karen?"

"Dale heard that there was a row, as he called it, so he figures that you have a motive."

"Because Matt wouldn't let Vinnie be my girlfriend? That's ridiculous. Okay, I did get kind of mad, but I wouldn't want to deliberately sabotage Matt's farm at all, never mind to such an extent that they end up in severe financial difficulties. I've known them all my life, and I haven't changed my mind about Vinnie. The idea of doing this to the family is daft."

Seb chewed his lip. Caleb was right. Matt and Karen would never agree to their daughter seeing someone who'd deliberately tried to hurt them. It didn't make sense.

"I believe you, Caleb." Seb was glad he could speak honestly.

"I'm glad. For a minute there I thought you agreed with Dale."

"What *were* you doing back in the parlour?" Seb asked. "I'm just curious," he quickly added.

"Once I left my phone there by mistake. I remembered about it when I was feeding the heifers, but I figured it could wait. The next time, though, I thought it had been in my pocket and when I reached for it, it wasn't there. So I went back to check the parlour, and there it was. I must have set it down without thinking, because I can't remember lifting it from my pocket."

"At least you found it and hadn't dropped it somewhere."

Caleb laughed. "You're right. Phones and farms don't mix sometimes. I've found that out the hard way more than once."

Seb chuckled. They ended the call and he set the phone down on the sofa beside him. He was glad that he had phoned Caleb. He didn't like thinking that the tall young man was responsible, but he hadn't been able to shift the nagging feeling.

Although they couldn't rule out that the rustlers were seeking revenge, it seemed unlikely. Someone would have noticed, or the dogs would have made a racket, if a strange vehicle had appeared in the yard. Seb was certain that all fingers were now pointing to Trevor. If only they could catch him in the act. Tomorrow he'd speak to Lavinia and work out a plan. Maybe Mum wouldn't mind if he stayed on here for a few days. He could always go home on Christmas Eve.

Seb gradually awakened, then stretched. “Ow!” He reached down and rubbed his toes. He couldn’t believe he was still making the same mistake after four mornings. Aunt Karen had moved Martha into a fold-up bed in Lavinia’s room, and Seb was staying in Martha’s pink and purple room, complete with tiny bed. He shoved the covers away and got to his feet. Padding over to the window, he pulled back the curtains and peered out into the dark yard. The snow glistened in the moonlight. It looked like there would be a white Christmas tomorrow after all, with more snow forecast for later.

He turned back to the bed and lifted his phone from the white painted bedside table. 5:22am. He should get dressed and start the milking. Caleb would probably be on his own this morning as Dale had been heading out last night and hadn’t planned to be back until late. Seb wasn’t sure what time he’d heard the stairs creak, but ‘late’ had certainly been the right word. He wouldn’t appear for a while yet, Seb figured.

The air was crisp and clear, and the icy snow crunched beneath his feet. Jess and Glen sleepily stretched and yawned when he poked his head into the shed where they were curled up on the straw. “It’s okay, stay where you are. It’s still early,” he whispered.

He headed into the parlour and turned on the light. He might as well make a start. Caleb would be here soon. As he made his way around the tank, he felt a sneeze coming on. He yanked a tissue from his pocket, and a coin flew out and rolled under the tank. After he'd blown his nose, he got onto his hands and knees to retrieve the coin. He bent down and peered under the tank… and recoiled in shock.

What was that? Surely it wasn't…

He sat back on his heels, thoughts racing like a nest of disturbed snakes through his head.

Who…? Why…? Gingerly, he reached in and pulled the clear package towards him. The contents were unmistakeable. A vial of liquid with a veterinary pharmaceutical company symbol on the side.

Antibiotics.

The door opened and Seb looked up. "Caleb, look at this."

Caleb frowned at the urgent tone in Seb's voice, but hunkered down beside him. "Wow!" he breathed as he saw what Seb was holding. "I guess we've found the hiding place for the antibiotics."

"But why would Trevor hide them here? Wouldn't it be easier having them with him?"

Caleb's face tightened. "Seb, I don't think it's Trevor. I was thinking about it last night and it's not fitting into place."

"So who do you think it is?" Seb's mind felt fuzzy as he tried to process what Caleb was hinting at.

"Someone who has access to antibiotics."

Seb sat back on his heels."We've been through that. You, Tommy, Trevor and Uncle Matt. And Trevor is our only suspect," he hastened to add.

"You've missed someone." Caleb raised an eyebrow. "Someone who may not have had access to antibiotics when he came, but he sure does now."

Seb stared at Caleb, the realisation flooding through his cold-numbed brain. "Dale?"

Caleb nodded.

Seb's mouth fell open. Caleb was right. Why hadn't he realised? Kate worked in a veterinary surgery. But would she really…?

"Do you think Kate would just give him antibiotics? I mean, from what I've heard about her, she's talkative, but not malicious."

"She's not malicious at all," Caleb replied, "but she really isn't the smartest lady I've ever met, to put it mildly. She's one of those types who gives blondes a bad name. And you know what Dale's like. He could easily have fed her some sort of story."

Seb did know what Dale was like. He had planted seeds of doubt in Seb's mind as to who was responsible. He shook his head to try to clear it. "We need to get the milking done. I'll put this back for now and we can think what to do as we work." Seb shoved the package back underneath the tank, lost coin forgotten.

As he worked, he thought about Caleb's suggestion. It made perfect sense. If Dale had been to see Kate last night, he'd have got the package then, and hiding it under the tank until he was ready for it was the safest place he could keep it. No one ever looked under the tank. Not regularly, anyway.

But why would he want to do such a thing? Dale was family, Uncle Matt's cousin and best friend growing up. Why would he want to harm them? What possible grudge could he have against them?

Seb closed his eyes as he tried to think. Had Dale ever said anything to indicate any sort of grudge against Matt? Suddenly, Dale's words slammed into his mind. '... Matt's always had it so good. Everyone hits bad times sooner or later.'

Always had it so good? What did he mean?

A dawning realisation crept over Seb's mind. Matt and Dale were cousins, their mothers both sisters of Uncle George who owned the farm. They each loved the farm, loved spending time there.

Yet Uncle George had left the farm to Matt. Not Dale.

'... buying a farm is well outside my budget... '

Dale's words echoed in Seb's mind. Dale wanted to own a farm. But his cousin had been the one who had inherited it.

Was Dale so bitter that he'd try to get revenge?

Or, Seb took a sharp intake of breath, was he trying to drive Matt into the ground so he could buy the farm he'd always wanted, at a cost he'd be able to afford? He could even make it sound good, say something about keeping it in the family.

Seb stood still, the clusters dangling from his hand. It made perfect sense. It wasn't Caleb, nor the cattle rustlers, nor was it even Trevor.

It was Dale.

The antibiotics were below the tank, everything in place for the final act of sabotage.

And this time, if he succeeded, Uncle Matt could lose the farm.

Chapter Twenty-Seven

"Caleb, when do you think Dale is planning to carry this out?"

The tall redheaded youth paused, a length of blue roll in his hand. "I think he'll do it this morning. I mean, he's been trying to frame me, hasn't he? In fact, he's likely overslept on purpose because he thinks I'm out here doing the milking by myself."

"I wonder why he just didn't dump them in the tank last night when no one was around?"

"He might be planning to put the vial in my jacket pocket. I always leave it on a hook beside the tank while I'm milking."

Seb considered Caleb's words. It made sense. If this was the final act of sabotage, then Dale was going to make sure that all fingers pointed away from him. They needed to be one step ahead of him.

"Caleb, I think that you should go home. I've been with you the whole time and I can vouch for you."

"But that will leave you with all the work to do."

"It's fine. Sure what else would I be doing on Christmas Eve?"

Caleb grinned. "If you're sure. That might be best."

Seb took a peek beneath the tank to check the package was still there, then accompanied Caleb to the parlour door and watched as he got into his car and slowly drove down the snowy lane. No one could accuse Caleb of being responsible for sabotage today.

Seb made his way back to the parlour and continued with the milking. He jumped when the parlour door opened and Dale entered.

"I saw Caleb's car leaving the yard." Dale seemed to be watching him closely.

"Yes, he had to go home early."

"I hope he's okay." Dale looked more irritated than concerned.

"I hope so," Seb answered.

They worked in silence, and when the last cow had left the parlour, Seb pulled off his milking apron and hung it up. "I'll do the feeding if you wash up."

Dale waved a hand in response. Seb left the parlour, and once he heard the thrum of the pressure washer start up, took a quick glance under the tank. Still there. He fleetingly wondered if he should take the antibiotics and hide them. No, he decided. Dale would notice they were gone and wouldn't rest until he'd pinned the blame on Seb. If they could catch him red-handed, they wouldn't need any further proof. Seb would feed the calves first and then tell Uncle Matt. Dale was probably going to wait until the feeding was done and Seb was safely back inside the house. He had time to decide what to do.

The noise of the hungry calves greeted Seb as he entered the calf house, and he set to work, feeding calf nuts to the older ones. He lifted the big yellow buckets and began to make his way to the parlour for milk for the babies. Halfway across the yard, he paused. He could no longer hear the pressure washer. His heart began to thump. Was Dale so desperate to sabotage the milk that he was willing to risk being caught?

What should he do? If he went into the parlour, he might catch Dale in the act and try to stop him. But it would be his word against Dale's, and he knew he'd try to pin the blame on him instead of Caleb.

Seb hesitated and glanced towards the house. There really was no time to go back and get someone. He was on his own. He wished he'd lifted his phone when he left his bedroom earlier. A video would have been indisputable evidence.

Taking a deep breath, he dropped the buckets and raced towards the parlour, slipping and sliding on the snow-covered ground. As he bounded up the steps, through the window he could see a figure standing by the tank.

Hand shaking, he slid the door aside, and gasped.

The lid of the tank was opened, and Dale was holding a vial in his hand, ready to tip the contents into the creamy, swirling whiteness.

"No! Don't!" Seb cried.

Dale looked up, a hard, cold look on his face mixed with shock at being discovered.

"Get back!" He snarled at Seb.

Dale was seconds away from sabotaging another tank of milk. Seb launched himself at Dale. The impact of Seb's body hitting the older man caused the vial to fly from his hand and shatter against the wall.

"Now look what you've done, you stupid brat!" he yelled.

"You were trying to sabotage the milk!" Seb shouted back, then ducked as a fist blow was aimed in his direction.

"This should have been my farm," growled Dale. "There was no reason why Uncle George should have left it to Matt instead of me. I spent as much time here as he did."

He reached for Seb, but Seb quickly sidestepped. There was barely enough room with the tank taking up most of the space, and Dale was advancing, right in his face. "And this farm *will* be mine," he hissed.

Seb took a step back, then another, and another. His back pressed against the wall. He held up his hands to shield his face. At any moment, Dale's large fist would make contact.

When the blow didn't come, Seb opened one eye. Dale had changed direction and was disappearing out the door. He heard the clang of his boots descending the metal steps. What? Where was he going? Seb took a breath, tried to steady his nerves, then charged after him.

Dale was almost halfway to the house, stride purposeful and sure. Why was he heading back to the house as if he was the innocent party? Was he really going to lead Uncle Matt to believe that the saboteur was Seb and that he'd caught him red-handed?

By the time Seb caught up, Dale had flung open the door and stalked inside. Seb followed on his heels as he marched straight into the kitchen and made his way to where Uncle Matt was lying on the sofa.

"What's wrong, Dale?" Matt struggled to sit up.

"I'll tell you what's wrong." Dale's voice was full of venom. "I've suffered this long enough and my time has come. Cherryhill Farm should be mine."

"What?" Uncle Matt looked astonished.

Seb could hardly believe that this was the same Dale that had been living and helping out at Cherryhill over the past weeks. He'd gone mad! "Uncle Matt, I caught Dale about to put antibiotics in the... OW!" he screamed, as Dale turned round and caught him by the arm.

"Shut up, you little brat. You need to keep out of this." Dale twisted Seb's arm behind his back. He pushed it upwards with a shove and Seb gritted his teeth against the pain. "You understand?"

"Dale!" Matt reached out a hand in a vain attempt to stop Dale, as he swung his legs over the edge of the sofa. Shock showed on his face.

"Understand?" Dale gave Seb's arm another push. Black spots danced in front of his eyes. He gave a quick nod, and Dale dropped his arm. It hung limply by his side and he rubbed it. The pain in his shoulder was excruciating.

Dale turned to Matt. "I just need you to agree to sell me the farm. Nice lowish sort of price. You're in big debt anyway, and beggars can't be choosers, you know." He gave a mean cackle.

"Now, Dale." Uncle Matt sounded as if he was trying to soothe an angry animal. "This isn't the way to go about getting a farm." He leaned forwards to pick up his crutches, but Dale's fist slammed into his face. Matt recoiled and his head bounced against the back of the sofa. Seb could see blood beginning to gush from Matt's nose.

Dale's fist flew forwards for another blow, but Matt was quicker and caught the blow in his open palm. He grabbed Dale's wrist and pulled. Dale, already leaning forward, was caught off balance. He fell heavily onto the sofa. Matt reached for his other arm, but Dale's legs thrashed around and caught Matt on his bad leg.

Seb could see Uncle Matt wincing in pain. What should he do? His shoulder was so sore that he could hardly think, never mind do anything.

He needed to phone the police. He patted his pockets. Where was his phone? He needed to get to the phone in the kitchen. He needed to do something.

Suddenly the door opened and Lavinia stood framed in the doorway, a look of horror on her face at the fight before her.

"Dale!" she screamed. "What are you doing?" By now, Dale had pulled Matt off the sofa and they were rolling around on the floor. Fists were flying. Dale had the obvious advantage, but Matt was putting up a good fight.

Lavinia tried to step closer, but a foot caught her on the shin and she leaped back. She looked at Seb, panic on her face. "Dad won't win. We need to do something!"

Dale pinned Matt onto his back. Matt was struggling to break free but was weakening. Lavinia gestured towards Dale. "Seb, help me. Grab his arm." She pulled one of Dale's arms, and Seb reached for the other with his good arm. Every movement made him feel as if he would pass out, but he pulled as hard as he could. Dale was much too strong for them.

Dale pulled back his hand and aimed a fist at Matt's head. "Are you sure you won't sell me the farm?" he asked menacingly. "There are other ways, you know. If you're disabled, you won't ever be able to work on a farm again. You'll have to sell, you know." Suddenly, he rolled off and aimed his fist at Matt's injured leg instead. Fear and helplessness rose as bile in Seb's throat. He felt as if he was about to throw up.

"*No!*" Lavinia screamed. Her scream was accompanied by a wild frenzy of growls. Growls? Seb glanced up to see two black and white blurs shoot into the room, teeth bared. In one move, they leaped onto Dale's back, one digging teeth into his arm, and the other, his shoulder.

"Ah! Get them off me!" Dale yelled, his face now white with fear and pain.

Seb looked on, stunned. Jess and Glen? Why? How? As he glanced up, he saw a little figure in pink pyjamas, clapping her hands excitedly as she watched the dogs paralyse the attacker into submission.

"Matt? Dale? Wh-what's going on in here?" Aunt Karen's shaky voice came from the door. Her eyes were wide and her face pale.

"I think you need to phone the police," Matt said weakly as he lifted a hand to his bleeding nose. "And maybe the ambulance."

The dogs were keeping a firm grip on Dale. They weren't going to let him go anywhere anytime soon.

Martha looked at her daddy and her bottom lip trembled. "Are you okay?"

"I'm fine, princess," Matt spoke from his position on the floor. Blood streaked his face and shirt, and his face was white. Seb hoped that the fight with Dale hadn't caused any further damage to his leg.

"The police are on their way." Aunt Karen set down the phone and scooped up Martha, cradling her head against her shoulder to shield her from the aftermath.

Seb hoped the police would hurry. He knew the dogs would hold tight, but the tension in the room was palpable.

"Get them off me!" Dale whined. He wriggled and tried to pull away, but Jess tightened her hold on his arm with a growl. Dale screamed. "I hate dogs."

"Well, I don't like people like you," Lavinia snapped back, her face red with anger. "How *dare* you try to hurt Dad?"

"And sabotage the milk tank," added Seb, as he sank onto one of the seats, taking care not to move his arm.

"You what?" Lavinia narrowed her eyes at Dale and clenched her fists. "It was you? You were the one who did it all along! And you tried to blame Caleb." She shook her head in disgust. "Unbelievable."

Finally, Seb heard the snow crunch as a vehicle drove into the yard. Still holding Martha, Aunt Karen dashed to the porch. "It's the police," she called, relief in her voice. She yanked open the door and stood back as two armed officers entered the house and zeroed in on Dale.

Seb watched as the dogs reluctantly relinquished their hold. Dale was handcuffed and led off just as the ambulance staff arrived to tend to Seb's shoulder and to Uncle Matt.

There would be a lot for the family to process over the next while, but for now, despite his shoulder, Seb had a huge sense of relief that the real culprit had been found and stopped.

Maybe now things would begin to improve for Cherryhill Farm.

Chapter Twenty-Eight

Christmas music played softly in the background as Lavinia pulled the messy silver wrapping off a pair of fluffy purple mittens. She smiled across the room at Seb as she held them up. "Thanks! These are really cool. Good choice!"

"Welcome," he said, ducking his head and glancing at Mum. She gave him a conspiratorial wink and he hid a grin. He was glad Mum had the foresight to do his Christmas shopping this year. He couldn't remember a year when Christmas had been overshadowed so much. They'd hardly had time to think about Christmas at all, and then when Dale chose Christmas Eve as the day for his last episode of sabotage, they might as well have cancelled the festive season altogether. If it hadn't been for Mum getting up at an unearthly hour to work on food preparation, they'd have been eating a lasagne that Aunt Karen kept in the freezer for emergencies, instead of turkey, stuffing and roast potatoes. Between the police questioning everyone, and trips to hospital for Matt and Seb, Christmas Eve had been a busy day and no one was in bed very early.

"I'm glad you're going to be okay, Uncle Matt." Seb smiled at his uncle propped up on the sofa. While he was bruised and sore, the medical team had found no permanent damage.

"So am I," he replied, as he worked a large, rough finger into a corner of the shiny blue package in his hands. "Thanks to Martha and those two rascals."

"How did you know to let the dogs in yesterday?" Seb asked his little cousin as he yanked a red ribbon free from a green and red tartan package.

She gave a little shrug and inspected her new doll. "Jess and Glen don't like Dale. I thought they might be able to help."

"And they did." Lavinia gave her sister a hug. "Good work, Martha. Maybe you'll be a dog handler in the police someday."

On hearing their names, Jess gave Lavinia a sleepy look and thumped her tail on the floor, while Glen stood up on his overgrown adolescent legs and shook himself, then tried to climb up beside Uncle Matt.

"Glen! Down!" Aunt Karen scolded, batting at him with a long, thin parcel. Glen turned his attention to the item she was holding and caught one end in his mouth as the room erupted in laughter.

When she had extricated her mangled present from his mouth, she marched to the door. "Right, you two." She pointed to the yard. "You might be heroes, but I still believe that the place for dogs is outside."

Glen dropped to the floor and let out a repentant whimper.

"Oh, Mum. Surely they can stay inside for one day," Lavinia said.

"It's Christmas," Martha added, her blue eyes pleading.

Aunt Karen sighed, then shut the door. "One more misdemeanour, and out they go." She wagged her finger to emphasise her point.

"Thanks, Julie." Matt lifted the book he'd just unwrapped. "Looks good."

"What's it about?" asked Lavinia.

"A true story about a Spitfire pilot in World War Two."

Seb looked on as Lavinia wrinkled her nose and Matt gave a laugh which didn't quite reach his eyes. Uncle Matt looked as if he had aged ten years since the summer. The weeks of relative inactivity had shrunk his muscular frame, and new wrinkles and grey hairs had appeared. The past few months had been hard on him, and being betrayed by his cousin was the biggest blow of all. Seb figured that Dale would have to pay damages, but while they waited for justice, the farm tottered on the brink of financial ruin. If only the repeat TB test in three weeks' time was clear...

Three weeks. By then, Dad's trial would be over. They'd find out the sentence that would be handed down. Seb hoped that he had begun to read the Bible he had sent him. He'd spent a long time marking different passages that he thought Dad should read, passages like Romans chapter three, John chapter three, and Isaiah chapter fifty-three. Passages which spoke of man's sinfulness, God's love and willingness to save, and Christ's death for sin. He prayed that Dad would come to know peace with God, even though he would have to pay for the consequences of the wrongs that he had committed on earth.

A hand waved in front of Seb's face and he jumped.

"Hello! Anybody home?!"

Seb blinked. "I was thinking."

"About anyone in particular?" Lavinia smirked at him.

He shrugged. "This and that." He wasn't prepared to dampen the mood, so he'd let Lavinia's assumptions stand, for now. "What were you saying?"

"I was just asking if you want to come and help Martha and me build a snowman."

"Yes!" Martha bounced up and down. "Then we can eat more Christmas pudding and custard to warm us up."

"More Christmas pudding, Martha?" asked Uncle Matt. "You'll burst if you eat anymore!"

Martha giggled and everyone smiled. The joyous strains of 'Hark! The herald angels sing' wafted through the room and Seb hummed along. It was better to dwell on the first coming of the Lord Jesus Christ into the world than on potential trouble. It was Christmas, after all – a day to enjoy. This was the first Christmas Seb had ever spent with the McRoss family. He bounded to his feet. And since it was a white Christmas, what could be more fun than building a huge snowman?

Sleet was beginning to fall as Seb followed Mum through the damp and slushy streets. He only vaguely knew where the Crown Court building was located, but Mum seemed to know exactly where she was going. They dashed through a gateway set into the black wrought iron fence and made their way through the revolving door. Inside, security personnel, dressed in shirts and ties, placed Mum's handbag into a tray, then sent it through a scanner. At the other side, Mum collected her bag.

"I think the trial will be upstairs somewhere," she said, glancing around the entrance area. The reception desk was straight ahead. "Wait here until I ask."

Seb glanced around as he waited. The building was modern and bright, busy with people hurrying here and there.

"It's the fourth floor," Mum said as she returned to Seb.

They made their way up in the lift, exiting onto a bright corridor. Court rooms lined one side, while the wall of glass on the other revealed a splendid view of various buildings with the River Lagan close by.

They stopped at the notice board and Mum scanned the listings. "Here we are. Alan Mitchelson, Court 14. We should maybe wait here." She motioned to a row of black metal seats opposite the court room door.

As they waited, Seb watched with interest as various legal personnel made their way up and down the corridor, black robes billowing as they walked, light-coloured wigs either on their heads or in their hands. It was like another world to Seb, for which he was thankful. He was pretty sure that if he hadn't gone to the farm during the summer and heard the gospel, he would have ended up in a place like this sooner or later. And not as an observer either.

Time stretched on, and Seb got up to read the notices and information on the noticeboard. 'What you can expect as a witness.' 'Do you feel vulnerable coming to court?' 'No mobile phones.'

"Maybe we should go in now, Seb. It's almost time." Mum stood and lifted her handbag. Seb could see that her knuckles were white from tightly gripping the handle. She was much more nervous than Seb was. She hadn't seen Dad since that night he left her for dead in her house.

They entered the courtroom through two sets of doors. The room was hushed and still, with a few official-looking people milling about.

Mum gestured to the row of fold-up purple seats at the back. "We'll sit here," she whispered. Seb pulled the seat down and sat. Directly in front of the observers' area was a large glass-encased area with a door to the left side. *The dock*, Seb thought. Beyond that were rows of desks and chairs, where a couple of the robed, wigged people were seated, and at the front of the room, elevated for all to see, was a large desk, which Seb figured could only be for the judge.

The room was bright, not as large as Seb had expected, and much more modern. Computer screens were plentiful and a large screen was attached to the wall behind the judge's desk.

Seb was inspecting the section of high ceiling in the middle of the room when he heard a sharp intake of breath beside him. Looking up to see what had caused Mum to gasp, he realised that a door to the left had opened and Dad had appeared, accompanied by a prison officer. He glanced towards them as he was ushered into the dock, his face totally void of expression, something that Seb never thought he'd see. Mum, however, was looking as if she'd just seen a ghost.

"Are you okay?" Seb whispered.

She nodded and attempted a smile. Seb figured she probably hoped it was reassuring. It wasn't.

Another door opened at the front, and a line of people walked into the room, taking their seats at two rows of desks perpendicular to the judge's desk, and then a voice called, "All rise." Seb scrambled to his feet with the rest of the room as a man bedecked with a purple, red and black robe and a wig made his way into the room and took a seat at the front. After everyone had sat down, and the judge had made a few remarks, one of the robed men got up to speak. He seemed to be trying to prove to the jury that Dad was guilty. Of course he was; Seb knew that. What he couldn't figure out was why Dad had denied it.

The prosecution counsel spoke enthusiastically and Seb tried to listen, but he couldn't understand much of what was going on, and the legal jargon was beginning to make him drowsy. He wasn't sure what Dad was making of the whole thing. He was sitting as still as a statue. Seb studied the back of his head. Large, balding on top, with wrinkles of fat around his neck, widening into round, pudgy shoulders. He wished he could see his face, gauge what he was thinking.

Seb shuffled and yawned, then immediately wished he hadn't. Even the rustle of his coat seemed to be as loud as thunder in the stillness of the courtroom.

Seb wished that he had been here for all of the trial. Maybe if he hadn't just jumped into the middle of it he'd have understood more. Mum had said that the trial began two days ago, the witnesses had spoken and today was the day they should be able to hear the verdict.

Seb's attention was drawn by Dad's meaty hand reaching up and swiping the back of his neck. Seb frowned. His neck had gone all red and blotchy and there appeared to be beads of sweat standing out on it. Dad ran a finger around the collar of his shirt and shuffled on the seat. The prison officer, sitting in the corner of the dock nearest the door, turned to look at him, and Seb could see a frown on his face. What was wrong with Dad? From what Seb could see, he looked unwell.

Suddenly Dad leaned across the seats and spoke to the officer. The officer's frown deepened and he slowly shook his head. Did Dad need to leave? Was he going to be sick? Faint?

Seb glanced at the judge, who was peering down at the dock through his spectacles. Even the prosecution stumbled over his words when he noticed the jury being distracted from his speech. Dad leaned forwards and put a hand on the seat beside him to push himself up.

The officer shook his head more vigorously and reached out as if to press Dad back into the seat. Seb watched as Dad ignored the officer and lumbered to his feet.

The judge whipped off his glasses, blinked and placed them back on his face. His heavy grey eyebrows lowered so much they almost covered his eyes. As the prosecution's words ground to a halt, the judge spoke sternly. "Would the defendant please be seated until the prosecution has finished summing up his case."

Dad appeared to take a breath, then stepped backwards. Seb thought he had changed his mind after all and was going to do what he was told, but then he watched in dread apprehension as Dad's shoulders lifted and straightened. He wasn't going to sit down. He was going to disobey the judge's orders! What on earth did he have to say that was so important that he'd interrupt his own court case to say it?

"I–" Dad's voice was raspy and he cleared his throat. "I would like to change my plea, your honour." The entire courtroom seemed to be holding its breath, shock reverberating off the oak wood furniture and bright walls. Seb glanced at the judge. Even *he* looked stunned. What was Dad doing?

"I've been dishonest and untruthful. And from now on that's not what I want to be like." Seb saw Dad's shoulders lift as he took a deep breath and then he spoke again.

"I'm guilty."

Chapter Twenty-Nine

"I can't believe he did that." Mum lifted the cup of tea to her lips. The liquid sloshed dangerously close to the edge and she tried to steady the cup with her other hand. "I mean, why would he want to change his plea at this point in the proceedings?"

"It really looked as though he'd figured that the prosecution had such a tight case against him that he'd be better pleading guilty for a reduced sentence," Seb agreed.

"Well, if that's the case, I'm not at all sure that it will work." Mum lifted a long, thin paper package of white sugar from the canister on the table and worked it between her finger and thumb. "He'd have been much better pleading guilty right at the beginning."

Seb gave a chuckle. "I felt sorry for the defence. Did you see him? I think he actually groaned out loud. Dad sure pulled the rug out from under him."

"He's likely giving him what for right now." Mum set the sugar package into the holder and pulled out a flat brown one instead. "That's your dad for you." She slowly shook her head and tapped the edge of the package on the grey plastic table top. "Never does think things through."

Seb lifted one corner of his mouth in a wry grin. "You don't say." Not thinking things through was what had got Dad into this mess to begin with. It was pretty odd though. Dad certainly had an impulsive nature, but another big part of his personality was a seeming inability to admit wrongdoing, or at the very least a tendency to justify his wrong actions.

Mum checked her watch. "I think we've time to catch the next train home if we don't dillydally. There's really no point in staying on today. We'll have to come back for the sentencing."

Seb popped the last bite of chocolate-and-caramel-covered biscuit into his mouth and stood up. "Whenever that'll be," he said ruefully. These court proceedings could be a slow business.

The courtroom was as silent as it had been last week, but Seb detected a strange, anticipative energy. Maybe it was the way the prison officers were leaning forwards in their seats, or the way the other spectators, young people, maybe here to observe before they chose a career in law, were whispering behind their hands. Everyone seemed to be aware of what had happened the previous week and no one quite knew what was going to happen. Again, Dad was in the dock, sitting straight and still. It was difficult to tell from behind, but he certainly seemed calm, and wasn't shuffling around like he'd been doing last time.

The judge entered, and again, everyone rose.

After they'd been seated, the defence counsel stood up and submitted a plea on Dad's behalf. As he listed various reasons for Dad's actions, Seb listened intently.

"This man was under pressure from others, not before the court, to act as he did... He was in fear of his life and ill-advisedly obtained a weapon in order to protect himself... He has no previous convictions for matters of a serious nature... He is genuinely remorseful and, albeit at a very late stage, has decided to be open and honest about his role in these offences, citing reasons of a religious nature..."

Seb sat bolt upright. Dad? Reasons of a religious nature? What was going on? He knew his father was no good, but to fake an attack of conscience and a religious experience was sinking to a new low. His mind whirled during the rest of the plea, and only cleared when the judge began to speak.

"Mr Alan Mitchelson, please stand up. I have listened to what your counsel has had to say on your behalf. You have allowed yourself to be influenced by others to bring a quantity of illegal Class A drugs to this country. I do not need to remind anyone in this court of the horrendous physical and emotional harm caused by illegal drugs, and you, by your actions, would have contributed to that harm. You also stand before me having pleaded guilty to the possession of a firearm, a matter of utmost seriousness."

Seb leaned forward, hanging on the judge's every word. The tension in the room was almost palpable.

"You have changed your plea to that of guilty. However, this was at a very late stage in your trial, and therefore I give you no discount for this plea. I sentence you to a determinate custodial sentence of five years, with three years to be served in custody and two years in the community. Take him down."

Seb watched as Dad slowly nodded his head, the wrinkles on the back of his neck working like the bellows on an accordion. Seb could hear Mum sniff and he turned to see her wipe her eyes. He wasn't entirely sure why she was crying. Because the sentence was too short? Too long? Or just the emotional stress of seeing her husband in court?

Seb wasn't sure what a normal sentence was, but he couldn't help but think that Dad had got off lightly. To be released from prison after only three years was nothing compared to what some families would have suffered had the drugs reached their target market. And what exactly would they do with Dad when he got out? The door beside him swished open as the other spectators left. The prison officers were leading Dad from the dock, and Seb startled as Dad gave a quick glance behind him to where Seb and Mum were sitting. He'd thought that Dad would look like his usual obstinate self, eyes narrowed and face hard. Instead, he looked peaceful, his face relaxed. Seb blinked, but Dad turned back around and exited through the door that the uniformed officer held open.

It couldn't be possible that Dad *had* actually become a Christian after all, could it? Seb gave his head a quick shake. Dad was probably just relieved to have the case over and have a doable sentence handed down. All the same, he was due to visit him again soon. He needed to find out how he was getting on with the Bible he'd sent him. Maybe then he could ask Dad a few questions, figure out what the 'reasons of a religious nature' were that had prompted the guilty plea.

"So how did you get on visiting your dad?" Uncle Matt asked a few days later as they milked the cows. With Dale's removal, Seb was back living at Cherryhill, but only until Uncle Matt got back to normal, which they hoped would be very soon. He was able to stand for periods of time now, providing he didn't exert himself too much.

Seb smiled. Dad had requested a visit as soon as possible, and Seb had managed to arrange it for the weekend. "Really well, actually," he said. He could still hardly believe the change that had come over Dad. Instead of mocking and sneering at Seb, his face had lit up with a genuine smile when he walked through the door and saw Seb sitting waiting at the table.

"Do you think he really is born again?"

Seb nodded slowly. "I know it seems far too good to be true, but I think he actually might be genuine. Time will tell, of course, and when he gets out of prison and the old mates start hanging around, it will be a good test as to whether he really does have new life. Being a new believer can be challenging enough anyway, but his situation right now isn't exactly normal everyday living." His mind drifted back to the visit at the weekend and he recounted the conversation to his uncle.

"I've been reading the Bible, son," Dad had said the minute he slid into the seat across from Seb. "Those verses you marked especially."

"That's good, Dad. I'm glad to hear it."

Dad grinned. "And that's not all. I was lying on my bed two weeks ago, thinking over my life. My grandfather wasn't a good man, as I've told you. He really ruined my childhood and I always swore that I'd never forgive him. That if his god was the real God, then I wanted nothing to do with him either." He'd scratched his balding head. "But when I thought about it, I realised that I wasn't any better on my own without God. I've been just as bad to your mum, and to you, as my grandfather was to my grandmother and my mum and me." His eyes had welled up with tears and he'd reached across the table to pat Seb's arm. "I'm sorry."

Seb had choked back a sob. He'd never thought he'd ever hear his dad apologise to him, never mind so brokenly.

"I really made a mess of things." Dad had wiped his eyes with his sleeve. "What you said that last day, about not evaluating God on the basis of those who claim to be His followers, well, I can see that.

I mean, if people judged you by the things I do, it wouldn't be at all fair, now, would it?"

Seb had given a little smile.

"Anyway, once I opened my eyes and let myself see that there is a God, that He's loving and kind, and nothing at all like my grandfather, it was easy to admit to myself that He's existed all along. The problem then was my sin. If there's a God, and I believe there is, then I need to meet Him someday. I know that."

"But you can–"

Dad had held up a hand. "I'm not finished. That's when I turned to those verses in the Bible. That chapter in Isaiah?"

"Chapter fifty-three."

"Verse five. I've learned it off." He'd cleared his throat before continuing. " 'But He was wounded for our transgressions, He was bruised for our iniquities; the chastisement for our peace was upon Him, and by His stripes we are healed.' My transgressions, my iniquities. I know all about punishment, but here's Someone – the Lord Jesus, God's Son – who took my punishment, what I deserved."

Seb had sat back, astounded. Dad was a believer? The miracle that he had thought would never happen, that he'd prayed for – hoping, yet not really believing that it would ever be.

"Say something, son," Dad had said, a smile on his large face. "Aren't you happy?"

"I– Of course, I just–" He'd swallowed, stunned. "I can hardly believe it."

"Think of what your mum will say." Dad had chuckled, then sobered. "Even so, I don't blame her if she never trusts me again."

"Why don't we cross that bridge when we come to it?" Seb had said, trying to form coherent thoughts in his shock-filled brain.

"That sounds genuine," Uncle Matt commented when he'd finished his story.

"It does," Seb agreed. "I guess I can hardly take it in. He seems really hungry for the word of God."

"That's a good sign of divine life." Matt reached across and pulled the clusters off the nearest cow. "By the time he gets out of prison, he'll have had plenty of time to read and study."

Mum had treated the news with caution, but Seb could detect an optimism now when she mentioned his dad, rather than a fearful dread. She'd even begun to talk more of the happy times they'd had, the small moments at the beginning of their relationship when he'd been caring and fun, that she had buried deep in the 'happier times' part of her memory. Dad still had to face the matter of domestic violence, but Mum hoped that he would be able to take part in a treatment program in prison. Seb had a feeling that Dad would walk over hot coals for Mum now that God had changed his heart.

"God still works miracles," Seb said, smiling at his uncle.

"He sure does, Seb. And even when He chooses to let us go through tough times, He's still good and faithful. Never forget that."

Seb knew what Uncle Matt was thinking about. Tomorrow was the repeat TB test, and with so many reactors last time, there were no guarantees that this one would be clear.

Uncle Matt looked at Seb around the jars of milk hanging from the parlour ceiling. "Habakkuk three, seventeen and eighteen, Seb. 'Though the fig tree may not blossom, nor fruit be on the vines; though the labour of the olive may fail, and the fields yield no food; though the flock may be cut off from the fold, and there be no herd in the stalls – Yet I will rejoice in the Lord, I will joy in the God of my salvation.' "

'Though there be no herd in the stalls…' Seb hoped that this would never be the case at Cherryhill, but even if it did happen, they would still rejoice in the Lord, in the God who had mercifully and lovingly saved them, and would carry them safely home to heaven at the end of the journey of life.

Chapter Thirty

"She's clear," Diarmuid called as the cow left the crush. Seb let out a breath, then immediately took in another as the next cow took her place. So far, over fifty cows had gone through and they'd all been clear, but they were nowhere near halfway through yet, and the chances of having a fully clear herd were slim. Seb desperately hoped that they could avoid the cycle that some farms ended up in, where they could never get a clear test. What they needed was a clear test today, and a subsequent clear one in sixty days, but how realistic was that scenario?

"This girl's fine." Diarmuid opened the gate and the cow sauntered out.

Lavinia herded a few stragglers closer and Seb gave the closest cow a light slap on the rump to encourage her into the crush. His cousin seemed to be avoiding Diarmuid – no standing at his elbow today. Thing was, the County Kerry vet didn't even seem to notice that the entertaining chatterbox was missing. It proved to Seb that what he had told Caleb was right – Diarmuid wasn't at all interested in little Vinnie, and she wasn't interested in him either. He likely had a host of ladies swooning over him in every village and town.

"This one..." Mirabelle. Seb's heart sank as Diarmuid paused and consulted the chart with the student vet that he'd brought along today, a slender, red-haired female. Seb fleetingly wondered if she was the reason Vinnie had been forgotten about.

"No, she's fine. Almost borderline, but fine." Diarmuid smiled over at Uncle Matt, who was directing the tested cows into a pen. Seb's shoulders sank with relief. He wasn't sure if he could have handled the news that Mirabelle had reacted to the tuberculin.

They worked hard all afternoon. Caleb arrived for the evening milking, and Lavinia didn't hesitate to go with him when he asked who was going to help out.

By the end of the day, Seb felt drained. His neck felt sore, probably from the strain of tensing his muscles so much. But there hadn't been one single reactor, nor an inconclusive.

"That's a miracle, Diarmuid," Uncle Matt had said when he shook the young vet's hand after he loaded his equipment into the truck.

"It occasionally happens, Matt. But I'm glad it did. With any luck you'll get a second clear one in a few weeks."

"That's what I'm praying for. God is gracious. We don't deserve anything, but He often gives us what we don't deserve. And what we least deserve is His great salvation which we can receive when we accept our sinfulness and put our trust in the finished work of His Son on the cross."

Diarmuid nodded respectfully, then opened the driver's door and swung inside. "See you around, guys." He closed the door and started the truck.

As they watched it drive off down the lane, Seb heard a faint, muffled sniff. He turned around and was surprised to see Lavinia standing a few feet away. She quickly dashed her hand across her eyes and blinked. Seb looked at her in shock. Was she crying?

Before he could ask her, she turned and walked quickly towards the calf house. What on earth could be wrong? They'd just had a miraculous TB test result. She should be over the moon – not crying! Seb glanced at Uncle Matt. He was still watching Diarmuid's truck drive down the lane, a peaceful smile on his face. Seb knew he was probably thanking God for His goodness.

Should Seb follow Lavinia? Would he be of any help? Maybe not, but he'd never know if he didn't ask. He spun around and headed across the yard. At the calf house door, the scent of calves, warm milk and calf nuts greeted him. Pushing open the door, he peered through the semi-darkness and caught a glimpse of Lavinia's red coat. Making his way across, he had to smile as he saw his cousin hunched down, leaning against the gate of one of the pens, the calf nuzzling her face.

"Are you okay, Vinnie?"

Lavinia looked up, startled. Her face was blotchy and her eyes were wet with tears. "I didn't hear you come in," she croaked.

"That's not what I asked," Seb said gently. "What's wrong?"

Lavinia lowered her head and gave it a shake.

Seb waited.

Finally she sighed. "It's what Dad said to Diarmuid."

Seb frowned as he tried to recall what Uncle Matt had said. He knew he'd told him that God is gracious and had given him a very short summary of the gospel. But Lavinia already knew all that. What her dad had said to Diarmuid might have been new for him, but it certainly wasn't new for Lavinia. "What exactly was it, Vinnie?"

She took in a wobbly breath. "About not deserving anything. And God giving us what we don't deserve."

What was Lavinia's point, exactly?

"I've just realised that all along I've been thinking that I deserve everything good that I've got. And I was really angry at God when it seemed as if He was going to take the farm away from us. But I can see it now – God owes me nothing. Nothing!" She paused and bit her lip. "And certainly not salvation."

Seb's mind whirled. Should he be saying something to her, or did she just need him to listen right now? He opened his mouth to say something, anything, when she went on.

"That's what I'd been thinking all along. That because I was a good girl and have never done anything really bad, that God owed me a place in heaven." She shook her head. "I was so wrong," she finished in a whisper.

"None of us deserve salvation," Seb said quietly. "We've all sinned against God."

"I know," she replied. "Each time I heard the gospel and ignored it, I was rejecting Christ." She stood up and rubbed the calf on the hard bump on his head, between his large black ears. The calf shook his head violently in response, eartags clattering against the bars.

"So..." Seb swallowed. He didn't want to pressurise Lavinia into salvation, but just realising how wrong she'd been wasn't enough. He turned to leave. "I'll give you peace to think, Vinnie. Come and find me if you want to talk."

She nodded, looking up at him with a tear-stained face.

Seb left and pulled the door shut behind him. Then he headed straight to the hayshed and fell onto his knees beside a bale of straw and asked God to help Lavinia not to reject His salvation again today.

Aunt Karen was pulling a chicken and pasta bake from the oven as Seb stepped through the kitchen door. "Ah, there you are, Seb. Just in time for dinner. Is Lavinia with you?"

Seb shook his head. "She might be a bit later. I think we should go on without her tonight."

Aunt Karen set the dish on the bench and glanced at Seb curiously. "We usually make a point of eating together if at all possible."

"I know, Aunt Karen. But this time, I think we should let it go." He desperately hoped that his aunt would make an exception for once. Lavinia really didn't need disturbed right now.

"Okay, then, Seb. If you think so." Aunt Karen looked a bit puzzled. She pulled a loaf of crusty bread from a paper bag and began to cut generous slices. "Is Caleb still around? Will he be joining us?"

"No, he's gone home."

Uncle Matt and Martha made their way to the table, and Uncle Matt gave thanks for the food. They had barely lifted their forks to tuck into the tasty bake, when the door burst open and Lavinia rushed in. "Mum! Dad! Seb! I've just got saved! I'm now a believer in the Lord Jesus Christ!"

Seb felt his face break into a wide grin. What better news could there be in the whole world than that of someone trusting Christ? Matt's fork fell to his plate with a clatter as he pushed himself up from the table and embraced his daughter. Aunt Karen followed suit.

"Vinnie," Matt said, choking through tears, "that's what we've prayed for ever since we found out you were on the way. It was what we wanted for you more than anything else."

Aunt Karen grabbed a tissue from the tissue box on the bench and wiped her eyes. "Oh, Lavinia," she wept joyfully.

Pasta bake forgotten, the family took their seats at the table and Lavinia recounted her story.

"As I told Seb, I thought that I deserved all the good things that God had given me. I even thought that I deserved salvation. So when all the bad things began happening with the farm, I started getting really angry with God and wondered if He was even real at all. But, Dad, it was what you said to Diarmuid, about God giving us what we don't deserve. I realised that I had rejected His Son so many times, and I deserved nothing but hell."

Matt nodded solemnly at Lavinia's words. "That's all that any one of us deserves."

"I know, Dad. But I saw for the first time ever that it's what *I* deserve. And then I realised that God had given His Son for *me*! I trusted Him, and I'm saved!"

"Praise God, Vinnie," Matt said, smiling.

"You know, this reminds me of the verse in Romans chapter two which talks about the goodness of God leading people to repentance," added Karen.

"That's me, all right!" laughed Lavinia. Her brown eyes sparkled and her face was lit up with joy. "God is good!"

Seb could hardly take it in. That his cousin, who only a few weeks ago he feared was turning away from all she'd been brought up with, was now his sister in Christ, on her way to heaven.

Uncle Matt was right. God was gracious. They'd been through so much, faced storms with gigantic, crashing waves and thunderings, yet, through it all, God had been with them, guiding, leading and protecting. He'd known what He was doing, He had a purpose in it all. And Seb was sure He would continue to lead and guide. He would be with them, both individually and as a family, right through until they all landed safely on the other side, in heaven.

And what a day of rejoicing that would be.

Epilogue

Five years later

"Mum? I'm home!"

Seb opened the door of the little bungalow and lugged his rucksack inside. The house smelled familiar and comforting, compared with the slightly musty scent of his student accommodation in Edinburgh. He loved getting back home for a weekend now and again, but it was never long enough, and in what seemed like no time at all he was back at the airport, boarding a flight across to Scotland again.

"Seb! Welcome back!" Mum appeared from the kitchen and gave him a hug.

Seb was struck anew by how small she was. She had always been petite, but he'd never noticed it growing up. Maybe because he'd been so small as well. Uncle Matt credited the fresh air and exercise, and plenty of good milk to drink, with Seb's six-foot-two-inch frame.

"How was your flight?" she asked.

"Fine," he replied. "A bit bumpy coming into Belfast, but nothing major."

"It was on time anyway, so I didn't have to wait around." Dad followed Seb into the house and dropped the keys on the hall table.

"Thanks for picking me up." Seb turned to Dad.

"No problem," he replied, smiling. "The least I could do for my favourite son." Dad had been released from prison two years ago, and since then had turned his life around. He'd found a job, took a driving test and bought a car, and was growing spiritually in leaps and bounds. He didn't even look like the same person either without the beer belly and excess weight.

"I'm sure you're hungry. I've made dinner and then we have to call round at Matt and Karen's house."

"Smells good, honey." Dad leaned over and gave Mum a peck on the cheek. Seb was glad that they had worked on their marriage. It hadn't been easy – Mum had leaned hard on the Lord to help her overcome her fears, and Dad had worked tirelessly to regain Mum's trust. Through a lot of prayer and dependence on God, their marriage had been rebuilt, this time on a solid foundation, and the day finally came when Mum trusted Dad enough to let him live in the bungalow. From what Seb could see, Dad treated Mum like a princess now and Mum basked in the attention.

"It's the spaghetti bolognese that I tried out the other night."

"The fancy one? With all the crazy ingredients?"

Mum laughed. "Alan, Worcestershire sauce is not a crazy ingredient."

"Oh, I think it is!" he teased. "I mean, it isn't even pronounced like it's spelled."

Seb dumped the rucksack in his bedroom and followed his parents into the kitchen. He could never have imagined, in a million years, that their family would be like this today. God was truly gracious.

After dinner, Dad helped Mum with the dishes while Seb unpacked, then they set off for Cherryhill. "Why are we invited to Uncle Matt and Aunt Karen's tonight? I was planning to go tomorrow anyway."

"I think they thought it would be nice to get together as a family for a change." Mum spoke over her shoulder.

"It is," Seb agreed.

As they pulled into the yard, Seb noticed Caleb's car parked to one side. He hadn't seen Caleb for ages. Seb's mind travelled back to the winter day when Lavinia had trusted Christ and to the evening a few weeks later when he and Lavinia, as well as Caleb, had been baptised. After Lavinia got saved, Caleb had returned to the Lord, and there had been so much rejoicing that three young people were obeying God's word. Caleb and Lavinia were still friends, but they never did become a couple, and Seb had heard rumours of a pretty, dark-eyed girl Caleb had met while visiting missionaries in Latin America.

Seb climbed from the car and they made their way into the house.

"Seb!" Nine-year-old Martha threw herself at him and he picked her up and whirled her around, her long, blonde ponytail flying out behind her.

"Hey, little cuzzy! Good to see you."

"Good to see you too, big cuzzy!"

Seb set her down and smiled at her. He'd never noticed it before, but she really looked so much like Mum. He hoped she'd make better decisions in her life than Mum had made.

Karen reached forwards and hugged Seb. "We miss you around here," she said.

Lavinia had risen from the rocking chair in the corner of the living area. "Glad you've condescended to visit us. You should come more often."

Seb grinned. "You're starting to sound like Madge."

"Oh no!" She laughed and her brown eyes sparkled. His cousin had grown up, but there were plenty of glimpses of the mischievous teen he'd first met. "You'll have to go and visit her and Tommy. She was asking about you the other day. Tommy's leg is giving him bother, and she's slowing down too, although she still talks as much as she ever did."

Beside Lavinia, a tall, slender blonde stood. Rebekah. Seb smiled. She was even more beautiful than she'd been the day he'd first met her, and only seemed to grow in godliness and loveliness each year. And, miraculously, still single. Maybe, just maybe, Seb thought, she might be the one God had for him.

He glanced around for Caleb and Matt. Aunt Karen laughed. "The boys are away to try out Matt's new toy."

"New toy?" Seb echoed, confused.

Lavinia and Rebekah looked at each other conspiratorially. "You'll like it," Lavinia said, smiling.

Headlights shone into the yard, followed by the low rumble of a vehicle.

"Go ahead," Karen gestured to the door.

Seb moved to the door and laughed when he saw the shiny electric-blue truck. "A new pickup truck?"

Matt hopped out and waved him across. "Come and see, Seb."

As Seb made his way across the yard, his eyes opened wide. "Uncle Matt! Wow! Where did this come from?" Seb admired the large truck with the big black alloys and chrome trim. "She's a beauty, Uncle Matt, but…" Seb knew that this truck was the top of the range. It cost a fortune. Financially, the farm had recovered from that difficult autumn and winter, but Seb knew there wasn't *that* much spare cash floating around!

"You remember Dale?"

Seb snorted. "How could I forget?" Dale had narrowly managed to escape prison, but had been ordered to pay huge damages to Matt. He was living a modest life, working in an abattoir a couple of hours away, his New Zealand life and dreams of owning a dairy farm in tatters.

"You might remember he had a sister, an artist."

"Uh-huh," Seb said slowly. Where was this story going?

"Well, she was so indignant about what her brother had done, that she decided to design and build a piece of artwork and give me the proceeds. It took her a while to complete it, but it turned out that the artwork ended up being one of her most popular pieces. She raked in a small fortune. She made one stipulation, though. Whatever I bought had to be something for me, and not for the farm."

Seb raised his eyebrows. "Isn't a truck useful on the farm?"

Uncle Matt chuckled. "Absolutely! But I certainly don't *need* a truck. The jeep was doing what it needed to do. Having a truck is a luxury. When I put it to her like that, she had to concede." He grinned. "I think she'd have preferred if it was electric and better for the environment, but they don't happen to do electric trucks of this particular model just yet."

Seb laughed. He wished that Lavinia had some hidden artistic talent – he certainly wouldn't mind a truck of his own someday.

Uncle Matt handed Seb the keys. "Go and have a drive. I've put you on the insurance for the weekend."

Seb's mouth dropped open. "You did?" He ran his hand lightly over the shiny surface. "Wow."

"So, get in, nephew. It's their most powerful vehicle to date. This thing can go!"

Seb shook his head in disbelief, but pulled open the driver's door and swung himself in. How different from the last time he'd driven Uncle Matt's truck, as an angry, rebellious teen, when he'd crashed it and could have been killed. God had been so good to him.

He turned the key in the ignition and the truck roared to life. As he pressed the accelerator and pulled out of the yard, he waved at his family and friends standing on the step.

They all waved back, their smiles illuminated by the glow of the porch light. He took a mental picture. Dad and Mum, their arms around each other; Aunt Karen, laughing at something that Uncle Matt was saying; Martha, waving frantically; and Lavinia, Rebekah and Caleb, smiling at Martha's antics. His heart felt ready to burst. How did he deserve such blessings?

He slowed at the end of the lane, then turned left. As he rounded the corner where he'd had the accident, just over five years ago, the answer came to him.

He didn't deserve anything. He was only Seb, a sinner saved by grace.

It was only through grace.

For God was a gracious God.

A Note From The Author

On that warm Saturday afternoon when I began to type what would eventually become Chapter One of Evidence, I had no idea if the words would ever find their way into print. And if they did, would anyone want to read them? Three years and three books later, I'm so grateful to all of you who have read the Search for Truth Series. Seb captured the hearts of a wide variety of people and many of you have expressed your sadness that Trial is the last book of the series. I have thoroughly enjoyed my time with Seb and his extended family, and I know many of you have as well. I would also like to say a special thank you to those who have encouraged me, either verbally or through messages and emails. It makes me feel very humble, yet exceedingly grateful, to hear how God is helping you by using the words that He gives me.

Trial, probably because there were so many threads to tie up, ended up with a plot with areas well outside of the scope of my knowledge. At times like this, I have to fall back on other people to keep me right – people like Michael Wilkie, who advised on the medical aspects of the story; Phillip Moore, who spent much time correcting my farming errors; and Rosemary Bailie, who was my very capable source on prison visits and court cases, and who even spent a morning with me at Laganside Courts so I could experience for myself what it's like to observe a crown court case. The book would have been much poorer without the expert input – thank you to all of you. So as not to lose the flow of the story, I have simplified all three of these areas in this book. I trust that those of you who are knowledgeable about any of these topics will forgive me for this.

Again, I'm indebted to David Williamson for checking out the apologetics arguments, and to Beth Herbison who always gives me an invaluable and very encouraging teenage opinion – thank you so much!

Others, who helped out in matters of grammar and punctuation, and made so many wonderful suggestions to help improve the story, include Margaret Moore, Eunice Wilkie and Joanne Grattan. Thank you immensely, ladies – I'd hate to release a book without it getting your seal of approval!

Samuel – ten years ago, when you promised to love, honour and cherish me, little did you imagine that reading and critiquing books about teenagers on a dairy farm would be in your future! Life holds many surprises, and I'm so glad we're sharing those surprises together. Thanks for your continual support on my writing journey – I couldn't do it without you.

Parts of this book were truly painful to write, and the sad truth is that while this book is fiction, some people are actually living through these situations. My heart goes out to those who have been or currently are affected by, among other things, farm accidents, domestic violence, and the potentially devastating consequences of a positive result in a TB test. Please be assured that God's love is certainly not fictional – the Bible is clear that He loves each person individually, and gave His Son to die for our sins. If you haven't already done so, trust Him, and you will know peace, in every circumstance, which only He can give, as well as the promise of a home in heaven at the end of life.

This is my prayer for you.

Resources and Further Reading

The following are either resources I used when researching for this book, or further reading for those interested in reading more about the reasons to believe in the existence of God, and particularly concerning the problem of pain and suffering. Please note, while these books can be very useful, I don't endorse absolutely everything that is taught in some of these publications. Another helpful, recommended resource is the website *answersingenesis.org*.

Hodge, B, Mitchell, T, and Ham, K. *Answers Book 4 Teens Vol 1.* Master Books, 2011.

Lennox, John C. *Gunning For God.* Lion, 2011.

Munro, Fraser A. *The Problem of Pain.* John Ritchie Ltd, 2016.

Randall, David J (Ed). *Why I Am Not An Atheist.* Christian Focus Publications, 2013.

Strobel, Lee. *The Case for Faith.* Zondervan, 2000.

Zacharias, R, Geisler, N (Ed). *Who Made God? And Answers to Over 100 Other Tough Questions of Faith.* Zondervan, 2003.

Scripture References

Page 18	Proverbs 27:1
Page 30	Philippians 4:19
Page 50	Philippians 4:6-7
Page 53	2 Corinthians 5:17
Page 54	Acts 8:26-40
Page 91	Proverbs 3:1-6
Page 117	Acts 8:37
Page 118	Romans 6:4
Page 119	2 Corinthians 6:14
Page 120	Genesis 3:1
Page 125	Galatians 2:20
Page 128	1 Timothy 2:4
Page 139	Mark 16:15
Page 160	1 John 4:16
Page 162	John 3:16
Page 205	2 Corinthians 5:17
Page 206	Ephesians 2:8-9
Page 217	Job 1 & 2

Page 258	Isaiah 53:5
Page 260	Habakkuk 3:17-18
Page 267	Romans 2:4

For more information about other books in the series, or to contact the author, visit:

www.ruthchesney.co.uk